SEP 3 0 2013

P9-BZR-970

FOREST RIDGE

TREES
WITH
BLACK
SNOW

FIERCE
DOG
GARDEN

R I V E R

TO
THE
CITY

THE
WILD

DISCARDED BY
CAPITAL AREA DISTRICT LIBRARIES

SURVIVORS

DARKNESS FALLS

SURVIVORS

Also by ERIN HUNTER

WARRIORS

THE NEW PROPHECY

POWER OF THREE

OMEN OF THE STARS

Book Three: *Night Whispers*
Book Four: *Sign of the Moon*
Book Five: *The Forgotten Warrior*
Book Six: *The Last Hope*

DAWN OF THE CLANS
Book One: *The Sun Trail*

EXPLORE THE
WARRIORS
WORLD

Warriors Super Edition: Firestar's Quest
Warriors Super Edition: Bluestar's Prophecy
Warriors Super Edition: SkyClan's Destiny
Warriors Super Edition: Crookedstar's Promise
Warriors Super Edition: Yellowfang's Secret
Warriors Super Edition: Tallstar's Revenge
Warriors Field Guide: Secrets of the Clans
Warriors: Cats of the Clans
Warriors: Code of the Clans
Warriors: Battles of the Clans
Warriors: Enter the Clans

MANGA
The Lost Warrior
Warrior's Refuge
Warrior's Return
The Rise of Scourge
Tigerstar and Sasha #1: Into the Woods
Tigerstar and Sasha #2: Escape from the Forest
Tigerstar and Sasha #3: Return to the Clans
Ravenpaw's Path #1: Shattered Peace
Ravenpaw's Path #2: A Clan in Need
Ravenpaw's Path #3: The Heart of a Warrior
SkyClan and the Stranger #1: The Rescue
SkyClan and the Stranger #2: Beyond the Code
SkyClan and the Stranger #3: After the Flood

SURVIVORS

DARKNESS FALLS

ERIN
HUNTER

HARPER

An Imprint of HarperCollinsPublishers

Special thanks to Inbali Iserles

For Isabella Maya

Darkness Falls
Copyright © 2013 by Working Partners Limited
Series created by Working Partners Limited
Endpaper art © 2013 by Frank Riccio
All rights reserved. Printed in the United States of America.
No part of this book may be used or reproduced in any manner
whatsoever without written permission except in the case of
brief quotations embodied in critical articles and reviews.
For information address HarperCollins Children's Books,
a division of HarperCollins Publishers,
10 East 53rd Street, New York, NY 10022.
www.harpercollinschildrens.com
ISBN 978-0-06-210264-5 (trade bdg.)
ISBN 978-0-06-210265-2 (lib. bdg.)
Typography based on a design by Hilary Zarycky
13 14 15 16 17   CG/RRDH   10 9 8 7 6 5 4 3 2 1
❖
First Edition

PACK LIST

LEASHED DOGS

BELLA—gold-and-white thick-furred female, Lucky's littermate (sheltie-retriever mix)

DAISY—small white-furred female with a brown tail (Westie/Jack Russell mix)

MICKEY—sleek black-and-white Farm Dog (Border Collie)

MARTHA—giant thick-furred black female with a broad head (Newfoundland)

BRUNO—large thick-furred brown male Fight Dog with a hard face (German Shepherd/Chow mix)

SUNSHINE—small female with long white fur (Maltese)

WILD PACK (IN ORDER OF RANK)

ALPHA:

huge half wolf with gray-and-white fur and yellow eyes

BETA:

small swift-dog with short gray fur (also known as Sweet)

HUNTERS:

FIERY—massive brown male with long ears and shaggy fur

LUCKY—gold-and-white thick-furred male

SNAP—small female with tan-and-white fur

SPRING—tan female hunt-dog with black patches

PATROL DOGS:

MOON—black-and-white female Farm Dog (mother to Squirm, a male black-and-white pup; and Nose, a female black pup)

DART—lean brown-and-white female chase-dog

TWITCH—tan chase-dog with black patches and a lame foot

WHINE—small, black, oddly shaped dog with tiny ears and a wrinkled face

LONE DOGS

OLD HUNTER—big and stocky male with a blunt muzzle

PROLOGUE

The air split with a piercing crack and thunder growled in the distance. Rain poured from the sky, rushing along the clear-stone in furious streams. Yap buried his face against his Mother-Dog's belly with a whimper. His litter-sister Squeak pressed next to him, trembling.

"Hush now, pups; there's nothing to be scared of." Mother-Dog licked their ears comfortingly.

Yap lifted his muzzle, feeling safer at the sound of her voice. For a moment, he was blinded by another flash of light before everything returned to darkness. His neck fur prickled as his littermates whimpered and curled together for comfort.

Mother-Dog scooped them toward her with one large paw, pinning them down and washing them with confident strokes of her tongue. "I know it sounds frightening, but it's only a storm. The Sky-Dogs and Lightning are play-fighting. To them, it's a game."

Lightning flashed across the sky once more, followed by another rumble of thunder. The churning winds howled overhead. It didn't *sound* like a game.

"But won't they hurt each other?" Yap remembered how Mother-Dog had urged the puppies to play together gently.

"No, they won't do each other harm. They're just having fun." She nuzzled each of the puppies in turn. "The Sky-Dogs were littermates, you see, just like you, and Lightning is their friend. Friends and littermates stick together through thick and thin."

"But they seem so *angry*," Yowl whimpered.

"Are you sure they're only playing?" added Snip.

"Yes, I am sure," said Mother-Dog firmly. "Now, my pups, it is time for rest. Soon the Sky-Dogs will sleep too."

Something in her voice made Yap look into her deep brown eyes as his littermates nestled together, close to the soothing beat of her heart.

She avoided his gaze, turning away to peer through the clear-stone to where the Moon-Dog had been before she vanished in the dark, wet sky. Was that doubt he'd seen in her face, or was it just his imagination?

Hearing the sound of his littermates' snuffles and snores,

Yap's head grew heavy. He wanted to ask the Mother-Dog more about the Sky-Dogs, but tiredness washed over him. He lowered his muzzle as his eyelids closed.

When Yap awoke the storm had mellowed to a steady rain. It was still no-sun and his littermates slept in a huddle of soft, warm bodies around him. With a jolt of panic, Yap realized that Mother-Dog was gone. He sniffed the air, locating her scent before spotting her nearby, a silhouette in the shadows.

She was watching the rain patter against the clear-stone, lifting her face to the sky, as though keeping guard. Her tail gave a small wag as Yap approached, and she turned to welcome him. This time he was *sure* he caught a worried look in her eyes.

Yap bounded up to her but stopped a few paces away. "Mother, it *isn't* just play-fighting, is it? There's something else going on. Something bad."

She lowered her head. "You notice a lot, Yap. Too much for a pup." For a moment they both lifted their faces toward the clear-stone, but the night sky was completely dark. "I've seen storms before. This one shouldn't be any different, yet somehow the air feels . . . *tighter*. The howls of the Sky-Dogs are deeper. Maybe they really are just playing, but perhaps . . ."

Yap watched Mother-Dog expectantly as she went on.

". . . perhaps they are angry."

Yap shivered. "Angry about what?" He thought for a moment. "Angry with who?"

Mother-Dog sighed. "I don't know, Yap. It's possible that a dog did something to upset them, and they want to remind us how powerful they are."

Yap's eyes grew wide. "What could a dog have done to upset the Sky-Dogs so much? And Lightning is a friend to dogs. He would never turn on us, would he?"

"You're right. Lightning and the Sky-Dogs are there to protect us. Maybe it's something else. No one has instincts sharper than Spirit Dogs. They could have sensed a threat. They could be howling to warn us of danger."

"Danger? But you said everything was okay!" Yap's tail drooped anxiously. "Why did you tell us that there's nothing to be afraid of?"

"I'm only guessing. There's no point worrying you when it's probably just the wind and rain." Mother-Dog leaned over and licked his face.

Yap pulled away and caught her eye. "But if there's something to be scared of, isn't it better for us to know about it? How else can we protect ourselves?"

Mother-Dog was adamant. "Fear does no dog any good. Whatever's happening, the Sky-Dogs will protect us."

From the darkness beyond the clear-stone, the air rumbled again, the wind rose, and the rain came down in sheets. Yap whimpered and hid his face between Mother-Dog's front paws. He had always admired Lightning, the brave, loyal dog who counted the Sky-Dogs as his Pack. Now Yap felt unsure. What if the Spirit Dog was angry, or scared himself?

"Don't fret, Yap. I'm sure the Sky-Dogs are just play-fighting. No harm can come of it. . . ."

Her words seemed hollow now, but Yap wasn't going to challenge her. It was better to believe that they were safe, that soon the Sky-Dogs would sleep peacefully. "They make a lot of noise when they play-fight."

Mother-Dog nudged his face with her nose. "Of course they do. They're the mighty Sky-Dogs. You wouldn't expect them to play *quietly*, would you?" She prodded Yap gently toward his littermates, trod a careful circle for her sleep-ritual, and took her place alongside the pups. Yap threw a last glance outside, where water was hammering down again. He settled next to Squeak, who gave a small snuffle but didn't wake up.

The wind howled, battering the clear-stone. Yap's hackles rose and he shut his eyes. He trembled as he remembered Mother-Dog's other fear—that the Sky-Dogs were howling in warning.

What could be bad enough to alarm the mighty Sky-Dogs?

CHAPTER ONE

Lucky froze, his legs trembling. Silence fell over the circle of dogs.

Alpha's broad, wolfish face was unreadable. He drew himself up on his rock, towering over the two Packs. By his side on the grass was Sweet, the beautiful swift-dog, staring at Lucky. Lucky could scarcely look at her.

Little snub-nosed Whine's tongue lolled and his jaws gaped. "You see, I was right! The City Dog was spying for the Leashed Dogs. He met with that one, the one who looks like him!" Whine turned to Bella, who glared until he cringed and cowered. "I saw them . . ." The little dog's words trailed off.

Lucky fought to keep his tail high. He could not let it droop in submission. That would show weakness—it would be the end of him in the eyes of this fierce Wild Pack.

They were all waiting for an explanation, but what could he say? He had spied on them, just as Whine had said. He had never imagined, though, that Bella would use the information he'd provided to attack the Wild Pack's camp.

Lucky searched the faces of the dogs in the circle.

What do I do now? If I show loyalty to the Leashed Pack, the others will kill me. But how can I turn my back on the Leashed Dogs? Bella's my litter-sister. . . .

He had been through so much with the Leashed Dogs. But the Wild Pack had accepted him as one of their own. He had shared the Great Howl with them, where Spirit Dogs ran before his eyes. He had felt the power of their bond, even as he balked at Alpha's strict hierarchy.

Then there was Sweet. . . . He stole a glance in her direction and she met his eye. He saw pain and confusion there, but also hope.

She raised her muzzle. "Lucky fought bravely to defend the pups from the foxes. Whatever he may have done before . . . he's no *Leashed* Dog. He's one of our Pack now." Her velvety ears twitched and she looked away. Her voice was uncertain, despite her words.

It's as though she wants to believe it, thought Lucky. *She wants to believe that I'm who she thought I was. . . .*

Lucky barked gratefully, even though he wasn't sure *where* he belonged.

He looked at his litter-sister. Bella stared hard at him, head slightly cocked.

She knows it's true. A part of me has grown loyal to the Wild Pack.

For a moment he felt guilty. Then he reminded himself that it was because of Bella that he had joined the Wild Dogs in the first place! And it was she who had brought the foxes into their home! She must have been crazy to trust those wily creatures. They'd betrayed her as soon as she'd led them to the camp, attacking Moon and threatening to eat her pups. He remembered how dogs from both Packs had broken off their battle to defend the pups when the foxes attacked them—first Daisy and Mulch, then the others. They had come together, repelling the vicious foxes. They had worked as a single, powerful Pack. . . .

Lucky noticed Moon and Fiery standing a few paces behind the others, their pups Squirm and Nose—the ones who had survived—nuzzled between them. Lucky's chest tightened with sorrow when he remembered the terror and turmoil, the frenzied barking, and the dogs who hadn't made it: little, helpless Fuzz, and poor Mulch.

Alpha growled low in his throat. "Lucky may have served our Pack for a time, but that does not excuse his treachery. What do you have to say for yourself, *City* Dog?"

Lucky licked his leg where a fox had mauled it, playing for time. His quick thinking rarely let him down, but this time he couldn't find anything to say in his own defense.

It was so much easier when I was a Lone Dog. A Lone Dog answers to nobody. But what if I'm not meant to be a Lone Dog at all?

Lucky swallowed, his throat dry. "It is true that I have been helping both Packs," he began. A growl rose from the lean brown-and-white hunt-dog, Dart, and was quickly echoed by the long-eared littermates, Twitch and Spring. They had been his Packmates, but now they were glaring at him fiercely, their hackles raised. Lucky struggled not to turn and run into the forest. If he did that he could never, ever come back. He had to keep his courage.

"I have gotten to know you all," he said. "And I've been thinking . . . what if my original mission to join the Wild Pack was *meant to be?* The Earth-Dog growled; the River-Dog revealed the path of fresh water; the Forest-Dog protected me on the way to this camp. At each turn I met friends . . . Sweet in the Trap House. My litter-sister Bella . . . even the Sky and Moon Dogs seem to have led me to this point."

Dart still growled, but the others grew quiet. Lucky could tell that he had their attention.

"See how the Packs joined to fight the foxes?" he went on. "Everyone had a role—not just big dogs like Fiery and Martha, but smaller fighters like Snap and Daisy. Dogs from different backgrounds, wild and leashed . . ." He paused, his eyes trailing over the assembled dogs. "You don't even know one another, yet you all fought fearlessly for a single purpose. Maybe the Spirit Dogs brought me here so that both Packs could unite?"

Alpha's face contorted in a menacing snarl but Snap, the Wild Pack's white-and-tan hunter, had a thoughtful look on her face. A few paces away, Moon and Fiery were still standing by their remaining pups. They exchanged glances and Moon stepped forward.

"Without the Leashed Dogs' help, we would have lost all three of our pups, not just little Fuzz."

Alpha watched her a moment and turned back to Lucky. The dog-wolf's yellow eyes bore into him. "That does not change the fact that he deceived us," he snarled. "Lucky brought danger and death into our camp." He turned his fierce gaze on the Leashed Dogs. "My Pack had to save this band of weaklings many times during the battle with the foxes. We cannot be expected to protect grown dogs who are feeble as pups."

Daisy bristled at this insult and Mickey scratched the grass next to his longpaw's glove with a forepaw.

But it was Bella who stepped forward.

Lucky's heart tightened in his chest. If his litter-sister challenged Alpha, she'd only make matters worse. He might destroy Lucky and throw out the Leashed Dogs just to teach her a lesson. But Bella dipped her head, addressing Alpha respectfully without looking up.

"I am sorry that I brought the foxes to your camp. It was unwise, and it was *stupid* of me." Her tail fell limp behind her. "I was duped into believing that foxes would act honorably. It was a mistake I will never make again. Truthfully, we wanted only to *share* in what you have here. We didn't intend to harm your Pack."

Alpha growled at this, his ears erect and his upper lip peeling back to reveal his fangs.

Lucky watched in astonishment as Bella lowered herself onto the ground submissively. With a whine she rolled to expose her belly. "I make you a solemn promise, Alpha, on behalf of my Pack. If you let us stay, the Leashed Dogs will serve you faithfully. We will obey your commands and fight alongside you, making your Pack even more formidable. We are better hunters than we look and we are keen to help with the tasks of the Pack. All we ask is to share in your food and water, and that you spare Lucky. He meant you no harm. He didn't know our plans; I swear it. And he did his very best to defend the pups when the foxes attacked;

the Mother-Dog said so." Bella looked briefly at Moon, then lowered her muzzle.

Moon whined her agreement. Guarding the two remaining pups, Fiery licked their heads as they leaned against his forelegs.

Lucky's heart swelled in his ribs, his anger draining away. He knew what it had cost Bella to surrender to Alpha in front of both Packs. He was sure that the last thing she wanted was to serve the ruthless half wolf. She was doing it to provide for her Pack—and to save Lucky's skin.

She hasn't deserted me.

He remembered her as a puppy, when she was still known as Squeak, bright, bossy, curious, and loyal—she had always been loyal.

Alpha shook his shaggy gray fur and scratched a large, pointed ear with a ragged claw. He was looking around at his Pack, gauging their reaction to Bella's submissive speech. Dart's hackles were still raised, but Twitch and Spring seemed more relaxed, and Snap's tongue was lolling from her jaws in a grin. Whine turned away while Moon and Fiery stood tall and gazed back at their leader.

Lucky held his breath, waiting for Alpha's verdict.

"I am willing to let you join us," the dog-wolf said at last, "but you will take low positions. You will be trained as Patrol Dogs and given the most tiring routines. If you believe you are capable of joining the more prestigious hunting group, you will have to *earn* that right through hard work and honorable combat. Those are the rules of my Pack."

Martha, Bruno, and Daisy turned instinctively to Lucky, used to following his advice. Lucky licked his chops. What choice did they have? Without Alpha's permission, they would not have access to food or clean water, which was in the Wild Pack's territory.

Before he could say anything, Alpha spoke again. "Foolish Leashed Dogs, looking to him. Don't you know that he's the lowest-ranking member of your new Pack? The *Omega*."

Alpha glared at the Leashed Dogs, challenging them to respond, but none of them dared. Lucky saw Whine smirk, his ugly face a crisscross of wrinkles. Lucky lowered his head, biting back a snarl. He remembered all too well the humiliations that Whine had faced as the lowliest Pack member.

But Alpha wasn't finished yet. "And the new Omega will be given a permanent reminder of his treachery: a scar on his flank so that none can forget what he has done."

Lucky yelped. He thought of Mulch, who'd been blamed for

eating out of turn . . . framed by Lucky and Whine, to get him demoted to Omega. Alpha had sprung at Mulch, scraping and gouging. Sweet had backed him up, adding savage bites to Mulch's wounds.

"Oh, Alpha," whined Martha, the huge Leashed Dog with webbed paws. "Be merciful!"

By her side, little Daisy yipped: "Please. Lucky will do everything you say; we promise. You don't have to do this."

Lucky whined softly with gratitude as Twitch and Spring joined the chorus of protests. "We agree," barked Twitch. "Becoming Omega is enough punishment."

Fiery cocked his head questioningly and even Sweet seemed unsure, though she stayed silent.

Alpha howled to be heard, his wolfish cry cutting through the whines and yaps. "The Pack will need stricter rules if it's to survive with all these extra dogs! That will be the price of Lucky's treachery and deceit."

Lucky couldn't imagine any stricter rules—Alpha's Pack was already so organized, the hunting and eating rights clearly regimented. A dog's rank even dictated where he slept!

Lucky had risked his life to battle the foxes, and yet the Wild Pack's leader was determined to hurt and humiliate him. His leg throbbed and his head felt thick and heavy, a grim reminder of that furious tussle.

The dogs were growling, barking, arguing with one another—divided over Lucky's fate.

"Wait!" snapped Mickey, the Farm Dog. He stood over his longpaw's glove, his ears flat but his head held high. "We're wasting time fighting with one another. We should be devoting our energies to surviving in this strange world, not arguing about who is higher in the Pack." Mickey tapped the glove absently with his paw. "Bella and Daisy are good hunters. The Pack would benefit from their skills. Why *wait* to use them?"

"Because we must have order," said Snap, the white-and-tan mongrel from the Wild Pack. "It's not about whether you *like* it—a Pack can't work without order. That's how it's always been." She spoke reasonably, without anger or malice.

Mickey's ears pricked up. "The Big Growl changed all the rules. Leashed Dogs are joining Packs, and Pack Dogs need to change too. Hierarchy doesn't seem necessary—not anymore. It just makes things complicated."

Lucky had rarely heard Mickey say so much.

Snap watched the Farm Dog, as though considering his words. But before she could speak again, Alpha sprang toward Mickey.

Standing over the cowering black-and-white dog, he snarled: "The Big Growl is an even greater reason to *stick* to order and tradition. The world is more dangerous than ever. What we need is discipline, not some lazy group of ill-trained house-pets." He lifted his muzzle, his yellow eyes cold.

Most of the dogs lowered their heads, careful not to challenge the half wolf. None of them spoke.

Alpha looked from each dog to the next, then glared at Lucky. "It's time for the marking ceremony. Hold him down."

Panic surged through Lucky's body, his legs trembling and his paw pads growing damp with sweat. His eyes shot across the dogs, wondering who would launch the attack. Several of the Leashed Dogs whimpered, but they didn't dare speak up for him anymore. Even Bella, who had risen to her paws, said nothing.

Sweet broke forward. Lucky yelped in dismay as she pounced at his back, hugging his shoulders with her paws and bringing him down. His shoulder smacked the earth and a twinge shot through his injured leg. His body crackled with fear and panic. Sweet was stronger than she had been when they had escaped the Trap House. Snap leaped forward to assist Sweet, slamming into Lucky and helping to keep him pinned down. Lucky whimpered as Sweet's teeth sank into his neck.

"Relax," she whined as he kicked and twisted beneath her. "It will be easier for you if you don't struggle."

Lucky's heart thumped faster in his chest but for a moment he froze, seized by panic and confusion. Out of the corner of his eye, he saw the Leashed Dogs cringe. Sunshine started barking in her shrill yap. Martha looked away with an unhappy whine.

Bella found her voice again. "Please let him go; this isn't fair! What is the point of injuring him so badly that he can't hunt or shield us from attack? What good will that do any dog?"

Alpha growled impatiently. "None of an Omega's duties are so honorable. I won't cause him any serious injury." His lip curled as he approached Lucky, who started to thrash again, fighting against Sweet and Snap. "Just a good bite. Something he will never forget."

The surrounding dogs were barking wildly, scared and excited, as Alpha stepped forward. He loomed over Lucky.

Alpha snarled. "Be brave, traitor. It's time to take what's coming to you." His yellow eyes glittered and he licked his chops.

No! I won't let you do it! thought Lucky with a surge of anger. *You will not touch me!*

He shook and scrambled against Sweet until she loosened her hold on his neck; then he growled as he threw his forepaws against her. Sweet fell back, stunned, and Lucky spun his whole body around, forcing Snap off his back. He scrambled to his paws and pushed through the circle of dogs.

He threw a breathless look over his shoulder. The dog-wolf wasn't prepared for this. Alpha barked in fury as Lucky passed Bella and Daisy, who made no move to stop him. Sweet looked surprised, even upset.

I'm sorry, Sweet. I just can't stay here!

Lucky hesitated long enough for Snap to launch a second attack. He was about to throw her off when a great weight fell on top of him. Thick brown fur with black patches obscured his vision for a moment, and then he looked up into the pointed face of Bruno. His heavy, powerful body pressed Lucky to the ground and Lucky yelped, more from shock than pain.

Bruno! But he's a Leashed Dog!

Lucky could hardly believe it. A moment later Sweet had joined him, her forepaws digging into Lucky's neck. With three dogs holding him down, there was no way he could flee.

The dogs surrounding Lucky were barking feverishly. Sunshine, the white long-haired dog, hopped and spun in panicked circles while Mickey retreated a few paces, his longpaw glove held protectively between his teeth.

Alpha's shadow fell over Lucky as he drew closer, baring his gleaming fangs.

"A traitor walks among us," Alpha began. "According to tradition, he must be marked so that all may know what he has done. As Alpha, it is my duty to make this mark."

Lucky closed his eyes. He promised himself that, however badly it hurt, he would never let them know it. He would not whine, yelp, or howl as Alpha's teeth sank into his flank—he would not give Alpha the satisfaction.

Alpha brought his face to Lucky's ear and snarled softly. "You can forget your life of freedom now. You will be known as a traitor for as long as you live. No Pack will ever make the mistake of trusting you again."

The half wolf dipped his head, about to bury his fangs into Lucky's fur and flesh.

There was a high-pitched sound like shattering clear-stone. The air felt cold.

Alpha froze. The sound grew in volume, almost unbearably sharp. It clawed into Lucky's mind and chilled his blood. Pressed against him, he could feel Sweet's heart pounding and hear Snap whimpering with fear. Even Bruno gave a yelp of confusion.

Lucky's eyes rolled up to the sky. Squinting, he saw only the pale blue of sunup. Then another sound roared through the air. It was coming from the direction of the city, sounding like thunder—but longer, lower, and more menacing. Waves of anxious yaps ripped through the group of dogs.

"A storm!" barked Sweet, her heart racing as she pressed closer to Lucky.

More high-pitched shattering sent tremors through Lucky's whiskers. It sounded as though the sky were about to fall right on top of them! A moment later the air howled so shrill and loud, it drowned out even the wildest barks.

Lucky was dizzy with terror, his stomach clenching and his flanks heaving. The sky was sick, whining desperately like a dog in pain. This was no ordinary storm.

The howling air had *nothing* to do with the Sky-Dogs.

CHAPTER TWO

Sweet released her grip on Lucky, stumbling back, and Snap and Bruno followed her lead. The shrill, high whining was still hanging in the air. Lucky shook his fur with a wave of relief, his neck and leg throbbing.

"It is a storm, isn't it?" whimpered Sweet.

Lucky knew that it wasn't. The sky overhead was still bright blue, despite the shattering and whining that sent quivers through his whiskers. No rain fell, and he did not pick up the scent of its approach.

"I think it has something to do with the Big Growl." Lucky didn't want to scare her, but he could not tell lies, either. That low roar had been like the sound the Trap House had made when it was falling down all around them—but much, much louder and far more terrifying.

The surrounding dogs shot him nervous looks. Another roar

of not-thunder made several of them jump. Daisy yipped nervously while Lucky tried to focus, training his senses, sniffing the air. He could just catch a strange smell on the wind, a hint of acrid earth, a tang of foul liquid. It reminded him of the poisoned river with its shimmering green water. He stepped forward, his jaw slightly parted, craning his neck with his ears pricked up.

Bella arrived by his side. "Bad smells."

"Yes," Lucky agreed. The putrid scent stung his nose.

The other dogs could smell it now too. The younger ones started barking, spinning in circles. Lucky's paws quivered with the intense urge to run, but to where? He wasn't even sure where the noise and the foul scents were coming from.

The frantic yaps of the other dogs broke over another roar far away, and Lucky turned to Alpha, wondering if he would silence them. The dog-wolf was frozen to the spot, staring into the sky.

"What's that?" Mickey yelped. Lucky turned to where a dark smudge was rising beyond the forest, his breath catching in his throat. It was like a storm cloud, but even darker. It looked more like the cloud of smoke Lucky had seen in the city once, after a pack of loudcages had attacked one another in the road and burst into flames.

That was where the foul smell was coming from. The city.

Had the earth torn again, as it had during the Big Growl? But they hadn't felt the Earth-Dog shaking. . . .

One after another, the dogs fell into stunned silence, taking in the dark cloud.

Mickey's pointed ears were pressed back. "Can it hurt us?"

Bella shifted from paw to paw. "Surely it's too far away."

"Let's not risk it," Sunshine barked. "We should leave."

"And go where?" asked Snap. She eyed Moon and her pups. "It isn't practical to start moving the camp, is it?"

"I really don't think it's safe to stay," whined Mickey, his dark eyes fixed on the smudge that rose in the distance.

Spring, the long-eared black-and-tan female, growled at him. "Go where you like, *Leashed Dog!* This is *our* territory and we're not about to abandon it!"

"I'm not scared of a cloud!" barked brown-and-white Dart, but her voice quavered and her tail hung low behind her.

Sweet shuffled her paws indecisively. "I've never seen anything like this. What do you think, Alpha?" She tore her eyes away from the dark cloud in the distance to look to the Wild Pack's leader.

Alpha was still standing on the same spot, his tail limp and his flanks heaving. Lucky watched the dog-wolf for a moment, amazed at his transformation.

He doesn't know what to do, Lucky realized. *Some dog needs to take control here.*

He turned back to the sky. Plumes of black smoke rose from the distant woods. The dark cloud was swelling as it caught the wind and seemed to be drifting toward them. It was still far away but Lucky could smell that it was filthy—even from a distance, the rancid scent that stung his nose also made his belly and chest heave. What would happen if it reached them? *Could* a cloud hurt them? Lucky had never heard of such things—but there had been a time when he'd never heard of foul water, and hadn't Bruno gotten sick from a poisoned river? They were learning new truths every day.

"I think we need to get out of here," he told Sweet. Several of the other dogs heard and they turned to him.

Twitch growled stubbornly. "It's our camp. We shouldn't abandon it!"

"There will be others," Lucky replied. "Mickey's right; it isn't safe here."

"What does he know?" Dart snarled, baring her teeth at Lucky and then turning to the rest of the Pack. "He's a traitor, after all. This is *our* camp; he can't just tell us to leave it at the first sign of trouble!" She looked to Alpha to back her up, but the half wolf stayed silent, still transfixed by the black cloud.

Bella turned to Dart and Twitch. "If Lucky thinks we should leave, I agree with him."

"He's not our Alpha," whined Twitch, "and neither are you."

Lucky was watching the black smoke twist in the sky, rankling at the foul odor that burned his nose. "The cloud is made of bad air. It will make us sick."

"Lucky has good instincts." It was Sweet. She had been watching quietly, looking from the cloud back to Alpha and Lucky. She spoke with authority, addressing all the dogs. "I know this . . . from before. If he thinks it is dangerous to stay, I trust him."

Lucky's tail rose at her words. He turned to the other dogs. "Twitch, Spring, you have the best noses of any dog here. Don't you think the cloud is bad?"

The dogs turned to the littermates, waiting for their response. Alpha didn't move, except for curling his lip scornfully, but his legs were trembling and eyes wide.

Twitch sniffed the air. At his side, Spring breathed deeply and winced. "Yes, it's definitely bad. You can all smell it, can't you? That's no natural scent."

Twitch sniffed again, his ears flicking back. "You're right," he conceded. "It's dangerous."

This sent fresh yaps of fear through the circle of dogs.

Lucky barked in acknowledgment. "We need to find a new camp, far away from here. Somewhere with better shelter if the cloud does come. We should leave *right now!*"

This time they all yelped in agreement, even Twitch. No single dog, Lucky noticed, had turned to Alpha for his opinion. *They know their leader has turned coward,* he thought. This gave him no pleasure. All he knew was that the new Pack needed to survive. *I don't know where we should go, but I know we shouldn't go toward the city.* He peered up at the tree-covered hill stretching away from the terrible sounds. They would be safer in the shelter of its high reaches and tall branches.

"Follow me! Hurry!" Lucky headed toward the hill beyond the camp, away from the newly torn earth and the black breath that burst out of it. Sweet was right behind him, Spring and Snap by her side. Moon carried Squirm, while Fiery scooped up Nose. The Leashed Dogs were on the move too, Bella leading the way. Lucky glanced back to see if Alpha would stay put, and whined in relief to see the half wolf following the Pack, though he hung a few paces behind the others.

Lucky wove through a row of tall trees onto a rocky outcrop, small pebbles slipping beneath his paws as he skated across them.

To the left, the land rolled steeply to a deep ravine. With a shudder, Lucky could just make out a jagged rock at the bottom, and a single, twisted tree stump. He could hear Sweet's light paws as she pranced behind him.

"Keep going," he called to the others. "Over the hill—don't look down!"

He raced up the slope as it bent sharply to the right, the ground growing softer beneath his paws. Burrs dangled from low branches, and Lucky ducked under them to avoid their hooked pods becoming buried in his fur. This far up it was easier to run, his claws finding purchase in the grass and mossy soil.

Eventually the hill reached a plateau. Beyond it Lucky could see a new part of the forest, and smell the fragrant scent of thick green leaves. He turned with an excited yap. Sweet and Bella were on his tail but some of the other dogs had fallen far behind. Taking a few paces back and around the sharp bend, Lucky saw that Sunshine was skidding on the rocky outcrop. Some of the Wild Pack dogs were also struggling—smaller ones like snub-nosed Whine, and injured dogs, like Twitch with his bad leg. Lucky scrambled down the hill, passing Alpha, who strode silently forward, his glance set ahead and his ears pressed back.

As Lucky reached Sunshine, he saw her skid backward, her

small paws scraping against the pebbles, unable to find a grip. A large stone became dislodged near her forepaw and rolled off the edge of the hill, plummeting into the ravine below. Sunshine yelped, scrambling away from the edge. She puffed herself up and tried again, pluckily attempting to mount the hill. Lucky closed his jaws gently around Sunshine's scruff and tugged her over the worst of the rocks. As he released her, she shook her fur proudly.

"Thank you, Lucky," she murmured. "I could have done it myself, I suppose, but . . . it's kind of you to help me."

"Of course," Lucky replied. She touched his nose before dashing after the others. Lucky watched her go. *She's really grown up since the Big Growl,* he thought.

A flash of the eyes from Twitch warned Lucky not to try lifting him by his scruff, so instead he circled the long-eared dog and shunted him along from behind until Twitch was able to climb the rest of the hill by himself. Watching Lucky in action, Fiery set Nose down. Moon gathered the pup to her alongside his litter-sister, who watched, wide-eyed.

"What's he doing?" asked Squirm.

Moon licked her ears. "He's *helping.*"

Fiery nudged Whine over the worst of the rocks without difficulty. The short-legged, snub-nosed dog mumbled his gratitude and continued his clumsy clamber up the hill, his flanks heaving.

Fiery yapped to Lucky and returned to Nose, scooping him into his jaws before he and Moon went on with the puppies.

Lucky looked back at the dark cloud, which was spreading toward the camp below. From his vantage point, he could see that it was rising from a valley behind some low-lying trees, probably not far from the city. It hung close to the ground, not high overhead as clouds usually did. But at least they were escaping it; soon they would be far away, building a new camp.

When he turned back to the hill where the last of the dogs was disappearing, Lucky heard a howl of terror.

It was Daisy! She was at the point where the slope crooked sharply to the right. Lucky bolted toward her.

"Mickey's in trouble!" she yelped.

The black-and-white dog had lost his footing near the top of the hill and was sliding backward. One of his hind legs dangled dangerously over the edge of the ravine, his other hanging on by its hind claws.

Daisy yapped frantically. "Come on, Mickey! You can do it! Just climb back onto the hill!"

Mickey clung to the trunk of a gnarled tree with his forepaws. As he started to lose his grip, dusty earth rose from the base of the tree. It was coming loose from its roots! He turned his muzzle away, his eyes wild, but he never let go of the glove in his jaw.

Lucky reached Mickey just as the black-and-white dog's other hindpaw slipped off the edge of the hill. Dart and Spring turned to see where he was going and yelped in panic when they saw Mickey.

Lucky tried to stay calm. He locked his jaws around Mickey's collar, careful not to shunt his friend away from the hill or cause him to lose his remaining grip on the tree trunk. Using all his strength, Lucky tugged Mickey back onto the hill. For once, he was grateful that the Leashed Dog insisted on wearing his collar—he was far too big for Lucky to tug by the scruff, as he had with Sunshine. The two of them collapsed in a pile on the dusty earth as Lucky dragged him over the last scrap of ground to safety.

Dropping the glove by his side, Mickey licked Lucky's face. "I thought that was the end of me," the Farm Dog murmured. Lucky could feel his whole body trembling.

Lucky nuzzled the Leashed Dog's neck and allowed him to catch his breath. Then he got to his feet. "Come on," he said, as though nothing unusual had happened. "Let's catch up to the others."

Arriving at the top again, Lucky saw that Snap was helping

Martha loosen a burr branch from her thick black tail. It must have gotten stuck there when the water-dog had turned the sharp bend in the hill. Once free, Martha lowered her large, gentle face to lick Snap's nose before turning to hurry through the forest.

Alpha is nowhere to be seen. He must have gone ahead, Lucky thought. Why hadn't he stopped to help the other dogs?

Mickey bounded after them between the tall trees and Lucky followed, enfolded in the sweet scents of the forest. In the distance, he heard the hum of the dark cloud as it pulsed from the ground, and another sharp crack had him bolting past Mickey and beneath the trees. Lucky zigzagged between trunks until something like a path opened before him, following the scents of the other dogs. He passed Moon and Fiery, whose pace was slower because each carried a puppy. Bella and Sweet kept level with them, looking out for hazards such as foxes and sharpclaws. Lucky paused to watch them, struck by how they appeared to have put aside their hostilities to protect the vulnerable pups.

Mickey sprang past Lucky, followed by Daisy. Most of the other dogs had pressed ahead but Lucky held back, remembering how the smaller dogs had struggled on the rocks. He had to make sure that no one had been overlooked. Retracing the path toward the entrance to the forest, he found Dart, the brown-and-white female from the Wild Pack. She was cowering beneath a tree, her eyes wild.

Lucky approached her slowly. "It's this way, Dart. Come and join the Pack."

Dart flinched, backing away from him and glancing in the direction of the strange black cloud. "The camp," she whimpered.

Lucky tried again. "There'll be another camp," he told her. "A better camp, with good air and tasty water. Trust me."

Her ears pricked up. Slowly she took a step toward him. "Are you sure it's safe in the forest? I've heard things." Her wide eyes shot across the shadowy branches. "My Mother-Dog used to tell me stories about giantfurs ten times the size of dogs with claws as long as branches and as pointed as a sharpclaw's."

Lucky shuddered inside but tried to sound confident. "There's nothing like that here. You'll be safe if you follow the Pack."

Dart seemed to accept this, rising to her full height. Her tail even gave a half wag as she took a deep breath and headed back into the forest, barking as she caught up with her patrolmate Twitch.

Lucky was about to join her when he spotted Alpha's silhouette some long-strides away by a towering birch. The dog-wolf was moving chaotically, taking only a few nervous strides before he would freeze, his ears pressed back, visibly trembling. Each time he stopped, he gazed back toward the valley.

Lucky heard pawsteps behind him, and caught the scent of his litter-sister.

"I wondered where you . . ." Bella trailed off, spotting Alpha. She followed Lucky as he approached the dog-wolf. Lucky could hardly believe that the fearsome leader of the Wild Pack could have been transformed into this fretful creature. Was he in pain? What was wrong with him?

He seems so feeble. . . .

Lucky had to remind himself that this was the same merciless dog who had relegated him to Omega, and had threatened to brand him with a permanent scar.

Lucky followed Alpha's gaze to settle on the rolling black cloud that the dog-wolf was watching so intently. He stopped dead, staring in disbelief. The cloud had inflated, twisting in the air.

Am I imagining things?

Four long limbs seemed to grow from the strange dark mass, followed by a neck and a thick black tail. The neck bulged into a head with long black ears. For an instant it looked like the hideous shape of a dog forged of ash.

Alpha spoke in a low, strangled voice, almost as though to

himself. "A Sky-Dog. An *evil Sky-Dog* . . . "

Bella drew closer, squinting in the direction of the cloud. "I thought all the Sky-Dogs were good."

"They said the same thing about the Earth-Dog," Alpha whined. "They said the Earth-Dog was kind and generous. That she would always provide for us, always look after us. But that didn't stop the Big Growl." The dog-wolf's bushy tail hung between his legs.

Alpha's helplessness had completely wrongpawed Lucky. He was at a loss for words. He looked again to the sky but the cloud had changed—it no longer resembled a dog. Once again, it looked like just a dark, floating smudge on the horizon.

"It's only a cloud," he told them. "Nothing to worry about. It doesn't *mean* anything. We should join the others; we have to keep—"

A loud howl rose through the forest—the cry of a dog in pain— and the three dogs spun around. Bella shot toward the sound, followed by Lucky and Alpha. A volley of high-pitched barks cut through the air. Lucky, Bella, and Alpha bounded through the trees, catching up with both Packs and running along the side of the dogs until they reached the front.

They stopped dead. Twitch was lurching in a circle in a

clearing between some straight-backed pines, howling in agony. He held his deformed forepaw close to his body, whimpering as he staggered and tried to right himself. His littermate Spring was barking, but the other dogs could only watch in horrified silence.

"What happened?" asked Lucky.

Sweet approached him. "There's some marshland just ahead, soft earth that's waterlogged and hard to walk in. Twitch tried to cross it but his rear paw got trapped and he fell. He's twisted his forepaw."

Twitch's flanks were heaving and Lucky was worried that something was seriously wrong. He looked up to see Sweet still watching him, her soft ears lowered. She stepped away from the others into the shelter of a low branch, and Lucky followed.

"It's the same paw that was already damaged," Lucky observed in a low voice. "Twitch is used to managing with a bad paw. He'll be okay, won't he?"

The swift-dog cast a glance at Twitch, who was whimpering pitifully. "I don't think he's going to be okay at all. I can't be sure, but I think I heard his bone break."

As she said this, Twitch slumped onto his side, his injured paw still raised protectively. He licked it, whining, his body shuddering.

Lucky glanced back in the direction of the valley. It was concealed beyond the forest. Above the trees, the dark cloud in the
sky hovered. Its body was spreading out and breaking apart, but
that didn't make Lucky feel any better about its presence.

What if Alpha is right? he thought. *What if the black cloud is an angry
Sky-Dog? And could Twitch's injury have been the Earth-Dog's doing?*

He had taken comfort in the thought that the Spirit Dogs
were watching over the Packs, protecting them from harm. Now
he wasn't so sure.

It was starting to feel like the Spirit Dogs were against them.

CHAPTER THREE

The dogs padded through the forest, twigs and dead leaves crunching beneath their paws. Their pace was slower now, allowing Twitch to keep up. The injured dog limped after the others in silence, holding his paw close to his chest. His littermate Spring offered to help support him but he snapped at her—"Keep away!"—and she took a few paces back.

Drifting to the rear of the group, Lucky studied Twitch from the corner of his eye. He wasn't sure if the floppy-eared dog would make it to the new camp, or how he would survive if he did. His damaged paw had already put him at a disadvantage, and now he would struggle more than ever. Lucky's own wounds from the fight with the foxes still smarted, and pain shot through his leg if he put too much weight on it—how must Twitch be feeling?

Bella dropped back so she could walk at Lucky's side. She, too, threw a worried look toward Twitch, and Lucky knew she was thinking the same thing. The Pack advanced without talking as the Sun-Dog bounded over the sky. The overhanging branches carved shadows in the light.

Lucky peered through the gloom. He had the uneasy feeling that something was creeping, lurking behind the veil of darkness. *It's this place,* he thought. *All these shadows make you imagine things that aren't there.*

A short distance ahead, the Pack had stopped. Lucky and Bella went to investigate.

Bruno was standing at the front of the group, where the trees ended abruptly. They'd traveled around the lake and now they'd come upon the shore. From here, Lucky could see the land curving around the shimmering body of water. He could just make out a large rock face at the distant shore.

"Where to now?" asked Bruno, looking at Lucky.

Lucky felt a wave of frustration. *This is the dog who helped to pin me down so that Alpha could brand me a traitor. If the black cloud hadn't appeared when it did, I would have carried a permanent scar. And now he's acting like nothing happened? Now he's asking* me *for help?*

"What do you think, Alpha?" asked Snap.

Lucky turned to look at the dog-wolf. He was standing a short distance from the others, gazing back through the forest in the direction of the dark cloud.

"How about over there, where the water meets the big rocks?" Bella barked. She was standing by Lucky's side, the other dogs converging behind her.

Lucky could see that the rocks formed an overhang. "Yes," he agreed. "Even if the cloud comes, those rocks should give us good shelter."

"But it's so far away," whimpered Sunshine. Her long white pelt was matted and dotted with burrs, and her tail was drooping. She gnawed ineffectually at a burr that had become lodged in the fur by her paw pad. The conversation reminded Lucky of the first time they'd left the city, when he had to coax the dogs every step of the way. *Not again! Not after everything that's happened.*

"Can't we stop here for the night?" Whine put in. "The trees will shield us from bad weather and the black cloud won't reach us here. It's too far to the rocks."

"We can't keep going much longer. It isn't fair to Twitch," added Sunshine.

The injured dog limped toward them. "I will keep up with the Pack," he sniffed proudly.

Sweet was squinting through the trees. "I think we should

keep moving. There are creatures that live in the deep forest, things that come out at night. . . . We need to be clear of this place by no-sun."

It was as though she had read Lucky's thoughts. He looked up, his hackles rising instinctively. The sky was dark blue overhead, the sun sinking low. "It will be dark soon."

Bella stepped forward. "Then we haven't a moment to lose."

The Sun-Dog was diving toward the lake when the Pack arrived at the top of the rocky overhang. Bella and Lucky bounded down the side, skidding on pebbles. The ground was damp, with grainy earth that clung to their fur in wads. Snap followed, scurrying toward the rocks. She barked encouragement at the others, still good-natured despite their long journey.

Then it was Martha's turn. With surprising grace for a dog her size, she glided down on her webbed paws as though following the course of a stream. Once at the foot of the rocks she shook her fur. The other thicker-built dogs had more trouble—although it wasn't as bad descending the rocks as it had been climbing the hill, most of them struggled to keep their balance.

Bruno half jumped, half tumbled over the pebbles, his paws

scrambling on the grainy earth. Fiery almost lost his grip on Nose, leading to a torrent of anxious barks from Moon, who was waiting for them at the bottom with Squirm. She nudged the puppy away from him with her muzzle, gathering both pups to her protectively.

Lucky turned toward the lake. "The water looks fresh." He led the dogs to the bank of the lake, where they drank eagerly.

Once they were revived by the cool water, the exhausted dogs retreated to the sheltered area beneath the overhanging rocks. The Pack gathered together, their mood miserable. Lucky's neck felt stiff and his leg still throbbed, but it was good to take the weight off it at last.

Spring lapped at a gash in her tail. She cast an angry look toward Martha. "That was *your* work," she snarled. The water-dog dipped her head submissively and took a place next to Daisy.

While the jagged rock overhead would protect them from the worst of any wind or rain, the shelter was far from comfortable—the earth beneath it was sandy and damp. Twitch limped to the edge of their new camp and slumped to the ground, nursing his injured paw.

"It's been a difficult journey but this will do for now," said Sweet, treading over the damp ground.

Spring yelped in frustration. "It would have been easier if

we weren't carrying unnecessary weight." She cast an accusing eye toward Sunshine and Whine, who stood next to each other. "Those two are too small to hunt or fight. What use are they to the Pack? We should have left them behind. They're nothing more than a *burden*."

"We do not leave any dogs behind!" snapped Sweet. "All dogs have a role."

Snap backed her up. "Not everyone has to hunt or fight. Sunshine and Whine can be the eyes and ears of the Pack."

"Sunshine has a wonderful nose," Mickey pointed out loyally. "She would make a good patrol dog. She can sniff out danger a mile away."

"I agree," Sweet said. "They can watch over the camp when other dogs go on patrol."

Spring narrowed her eyes. Whine glanced about fearfully, his short tail curling between his legs.

Sunshine wasn't so easily silenced. "Who are you calling a burden?" she growled, glaring at Spring. "I didn't see you fighting so courageously with the foxes. You bark and make a lot of big noise, but when it comes right down to it—"

"How dare you!" howled Spring, leaping toward Sunshine with her teeth bared.

Sweet moved to block her. "Enough! Both of you, stop it—right now!" she snarled.

Spring fell back, hackles still raised but head dipped. "Sorry, Beta," she murmured, unwilling to challenge Alpha's second-in-command. Appearing from the shadows beyond the rocks, Alpha himself sauntered toward them, staring down his nose at Spring.

"Squabbles. Pointless squabbles." He turned away with a dismissive flick of the tail.

Lucky stared at him, amazed by the change in the dog-wolf's demeanor.

It's as though nothing happened.

Sunshine swallowed a yap, glaring at Spring, but Twitch's litter-sister was looking elsewhere.

"Where's he off to now?" she barked loudly.

The dogs turned to see Whine slipping out of the camp. He spun around guiltily.

"Try to run away, would you?" Spring accused. "What a coward!"

"Coward! Coward!" yapped some of the others, their exhaustion turning to frustration.

Bruno snapped at Whine as he slunk past, nipping him on his flank. It wasn't a deep bite, but Whine yelped and scrambled beneath the overhang, shrinking against the wall.

"Stop that at once!" Bella barked at Bruno, who reared away from the little snub-nosed dog.

Lucky watched with his ears pressed flat. In the desperate time after the air had whined and acrid smoke rose in the distance, the dogs had set aside rank and rivalry to get everyone safely away from the old camp. But now the dogs were turning on one another again, forgetting how well they had worked together as a Pack.

Twitch kept away from the others, his tail limp at his side as he tended to his bad paw. Lucky noticed Dart speaking to Sweet, both of them looking troubled—though he couldn't hear what they were saying. Sweet glanced up and met Lucky's eyes with a wary, uncertain look. Lucky tipped his head to one side.

Will Sweet ever forgive me for helping the Leashed Dogs? he wondered.

Moon was nursing her pups as Fiery stood by, making sure that the bickering dogs didn't come too close. Alpha pushed past them.

"Settle down, all of you! Your whines are growing tedious." Alpha directed this order at Bruno and some of the others, but Fiery bristled.

Nose panicked at Alpha's loud voice, trembling and yipping. Both pups refused to suckle, despite Moon's gentle coaxing. Her dark eyes, wide with distress, shot to Fiery.

Lucky saw something pass between them; then Fiery turned to Alpha. "Careful," he growled. "You're upsetting the pups, putting them off their feeding."

The half wolf's head snapped back and he locked eyes with Fiery. The stocky brown dog rose to his full height, his ears pricked forward and his tail jutting out, as though he was about to challenge their leader.

Lucky's belly burned with unease. This was dangerous. A conflict between Alpha and a rival dog—especially one as powerful as Fiery, who was already only a few ranks below the Alpha position—could completely unbalance the Pack.

There would be torn allegiances, combat, bloodshed . . .

Alpha and Fiery stared at each other for a few moments as the others watched in anxious silence. Then Fiery looked away, dropping his head. Alpha snarled in warning and Fiery lowered his hackles and took a step back. Satisfied, the Pack leader raised his muzzle and glanced around the surrounding dogs in challenge. No one met his eye.

Daisy sidled up to Lucky. "Why does everything have to be so hard? Each time we get settled, something happens that forces us to move on. It's cold here, and we haven't eaten all sun-high." She gazed at him sadly, her ears drooping.

Lucky licked her ears and tried to soothe her. "Give it a chance," he told her. "I know it seems a bit unfriendly here, but we're safe from the cloud and near fresh water. Tomorrow will be better."

Mickey had overheard him and whined unhappily: "All we do is run and hide. We form camps but then have to move on, constantly looking over our backs to invisible dangers. It wasn't like this in the city."

"But the city is the most dangerous place of all," yelped Daisy sadly.

"It might be safe now." Mickey tapped the leather glove with his forepaw. "Did you see that black cloud? It wasn't just a shapeless thing."

Lucky's ears pricked up. Had Mickey also observed the figure of a dog in the sky?

"Didn't you notice anything unusual about it?" Mickey's tail started wagging. "It was the shape of a giant longpaw. It was a master's paw *pointing*!"

Several of the Leashed Dogs crept toward him, listening intently. It hadn't looked like a longpaw to Lucky, but he didn't interrupt.

"It's like the safe caves by the river," said Mickey. "It's a sign.

Our longpaws were pointing the way *back* to the city." His voice rose in excitement, his tail lashing the air. "They want us to come home. Maybe they've returned!"

Alpha stalked between the dogs, pushing his way to the front of the group. Lucky watched him suspiciously—where had this kind of confidence been when it *mattered*? He remembered how the half wolf had cowered beneath the black cloud. Now he was strutting around as though he had been in complete control the whole time.

"Longpaws, longpaws, longpaws—that's all you Leashed Dogs ever talk about! Do you have any idea how ridiculous you sound? You especially, Farm Dog." He glared at Mickey with disgust. "Why are you still carrying around that strange longpaw thing? Isn't it time to get rid of it?" Alpha sniffed the glove and Mickey snatched it up in his jaws, stepping back and holding it close. Alpha's lip curled as he growled: "If you're so keen to get back to your masters, why not run away to the city? We don't want Leashed Dogs here."

Mickey dropped the glove between his forepaws.

"Good idea!" he replied. He turned to the other Leashed Dogs. "It's time to go back to the city—time to find our long-paws. Who's with me?" Mickey cast his eyes around the group of dogs. While a couple of the Leashed Dogs whimpered, none would meet his gaze. Martha licked her feathery tail, removing the last of the burrs. Daisy gazed out beneath the overhang to the peaceful lake. A long silence followed while Lucky stared at his paws, not sure what to say.

Mickey's ears flicked back. "I don't care what you think. I know they've returned. I'll go alone if I have to!" He scooped up the glove and started along the shore of the lake, toward the place where the Sun-Dog was settling to his rest beyond the horizon. It was almost dark out there.

Lucky stood in his way. "Don't do this," he whined. "We've only just escaped all the danger that's behind us, and now you're planning to retrace your steps to the city? Even traveling in a Pack we didn't escape unscathed." Lucky thought sadly of Alfie, who had almost died when his longpaws' house collapsed . . . and who had been killed in a fight between the Packs. Killed by Alpha.

Daisy caught up with them. "Please don't go," she whimpered.

Mickey was resolute. He dropped the glove so he could speak. "I don't belong here. I don't like all the arguments, all the troubles in Pack life. I need to leave. My longpaw is waiting for me. I can feel it."

Lucky growled. "It isn't safe for you to travel alone. I won't let you!" He squared up to the black-and-white dog, his body stiff.

"You can't stop me," said Mickey. He shoved past as Lucky looked on, tail lowered. Then he paused and turned. His face was softer now, his brown eyes warm.

Lucky's tail thrashed happily.

He's changed his mind!

Mickey stepped forward, dropping his glove to lick Lucky's muzzle. Then he turned to Martha and Daisy and did the same.

Little Sunshine yipped, bounding out from beneath the rocky overhang.

Mickey lowered his head and licked her white ears. "I hadn't forgotten you," he murmured.

Lucky's tail sank. "You're still going?"

Mickey turned to him. "I have to."

This time Lucky didn't try to stop him. He stood between Martha and Daisy, watching as Mickey picked up his glove and turned away from them one more time.

The last time, Lucky thought, sadness like a claw lodged in his flesh.

The Farm Dog's outline soon merged with the creeping darkness. Several of the Leashed Dogs stood a while longer, but Lucky returned to the camp beneath the rocks and sank to the floor, listening to his friend's retreating pawsteps. The crunch of stones on the rocky path disappeared as Mickey scrambled up the rock shaft. Then there was only the rippling water on the lake and the wind in the cool night air.

CHAPTER FOUR

Dogs snarled and spat at one another, tearing at one another's throats under a boiling black sky.

But this was no honest battle of Pack versus Pack. Litter-siblings had turned against one another. Dogs who had fought side by side bit and clawed indiscriminately at their comrades.

Is this the Storm of Dogs? When Packs tear themselves apart?

Lucky barked desperately, pleading with the shadowy dogs to cease their battle.

We must stick together!

But the fighting went on and on, until the field was soaked in the blood of friend and enemy alike. . . .

Lucky's eyes flicked open and his ears pricked up as he awoke to the sound of angry growls. Looking around, it took him a moment to remember where he was. The Sun-Dog was rising behind the valley and touching the lake in the distance with shimmers of light.

Beneath the rocks it was shadowy and cool. Most of the dogs were still sleeping, curled up close to one another for warmth. Lucky got to his paws with a yawn and stretched. He felt stiff and tired. His head and hind leg still ached from the clash with the foxes.

Then he heard a growl. Just beyond the rocks he saw Bella and Sweet. He couldn't make out exactly what they were saying but by their postures he knew that their peace had been short-lived. He stepped warily around the sleeping dogs and out into the low light of sunup.

Sweet was snarling at Bella as Lucky approached. "Your Pack has brought us nothing but trouble since the moment you arrived in our territory. You'd better get out of here before everything falls to pieces!"

Bella did not budge. "It isn't my fault, or the fault of my Pack, that Twitch decided to leave. We slowed down for him. We tried to help him. He was with *you* when he got hurt."

Sweet growled angrily at this but Lucky interrupted:

"What happened to Twitch?"

Sweet turned to look at him, her eyes cool. "He disappeared in the middle of the night. Nobody knows where he went."

Lucky absorbed this news with a shiver of dread. He thought of the unhappy dog with the injured paw. Twitch had struggled to make his way through the forest last night and had scarcely managed the descent by the lake. How would he fare out there in the wild, where foxes and other creatures stalked? How could he hunt? How would he survive?

Lucky was snapped out of these thoughts by Sweet barking at Bella: "We don't know where Twitch has gone." She had inched closer, her narrow body bolt upright, her lips curled back. "But in a way, he's shown us what to do. Look at this place. I've scarcely seen a living thing all morning. The grass is sandy and damp. There won't be enough food for all these dogs." She glared accusingly at Daisy and Martha, who had gathered with some of the Wild Pack to watch the exchange from the distance of the rock cover, their tails low. "Maybe back at our own camp we could have supported you, but the Pack is too big for a place like this." She turned to Bella. "It's time for the Leashed Dogs to stand on their own four paws. You should move on to establish your own camp—*somewhere else.*"

Daisy and Martha exchanged worried looks. Standing behind them, Bruno, Snap, and Fiery looked on warily.

Bella ignored them. She would not be cowed. "Aren't you rather full of yourself, Beta? It was *Lucky* who spotted the dark cloud and helped the Pack to safety—and in case you've forgotten, he's one of us. You *need* the Leashed Dogs."

Lucky's fur prickled uncomfortably. It wasn't fair of Bella to bring him into this. He didn't want Sweet to be reminded of his betrayal!

Alpha appeared from behind the rocks, a shock of gray fur. He sprang down toward them and landed between Bella and Sweet, who both started back in surprise.

"Arguing won't help anyone." He paced between Bella and Sweet, his head held high. Lucky would have expected Alpha to take Sweet's side, but his voice was actually level—reasonable. "There are a lot of nervous dogs in the bigger Pack now. Their courage will hardly be aided by this display of aggression between the stronger among us."

Lucky tried not to let his amazement show. *You're talking about courage?* he thought. *After your performance?*

"You need to remember," Alpha went on, "that these weaker dogs look up to you. You are my Beta. The Pack respects you." He threw a dubious look at Bella. "And your dogs look up to you, too, I imagine. You must both demonstrate that you have courage and good sense. That you won't compromise the security of the others by being reckless or selfish . . . the way *Omega* was."

Lucky froze, his tail stiffening behind him. *What does he mean by that?*

Alpha stood up straight, his yellow eyes glinting with confidence. "All the bad things that have fallen upon the Pack happened *after* Omega showed up." The dog-wolf turned to Lucky and narrowed his eyes accusingly. "We're stronger together but not with the *City Dog* around."

"But the *cloud* wasn't Lucky's fault," Bella said in a reasonable voice.

Alpha turned to her. "You will address him by his proper name," he growled. "And whether or not Omega caused the black cloud, it took the shape of a Sky-Dog. I have no doubt of that. You saw it too!"

Sweet stared at Alpha. "A Sky-Dog? What do you mean?" She hadn't been there when Lucky and Bella had watched with Alpha as the cloud seemed to assume the form of a dog. She hadn't witnessed Alpha's panic and horrified certainty that an evil Sky-Dog was to blame for their miseries.

"The black cloud was a Sky-Dog," Alpha barked. "I would not be surprised if his rage was punishment for Omega's deceit in playing the two Packs against each other."

Lucky felt the blood drain away from him and he caught his breath. He'd heard that the Spirit Dogs could turn on a dog in anger. Hadn't his Mother-Dog told him so when he was only a pup?

Could this have been my fault? Lucky's eyes shot to the sky, where the black cloud was concealed beyond the forest.

The dogs watching from beneath the rocky overhang had crept forward, anxious to understand what was going on. Alpha turned to acknowledge them.

"I have made my decision," he said. "I will keep my word and not force the Leashed Dogs to leave. They may still have a role to play in this Pack. It is a dangerous, unknown world that we face, and it will be safer if we stick together." He spoke softly, but with authority, like a gentle Father-Dog giving his helpless pups an important lesson. "But Lucky cannot be part of this Pack, even as Omega. Look at the trouble he causes—conflict follows him like his own tail."

Alpha turned back to Sweet and Bella, making a show of ignoring eye contact with Lucky. "You have both spoken up for Omega, as though he is your ally. But he has brought you to constant bickering. He is at the center of all that has gone wrong for both our Packs."

Lucky's moment of doubt had passed. He was *not* responsible for the dark cloud. Whatever it was, it was somehow linked to the strange, changed world that the Big Growl had left behind. *Alpha's just using it as an excuse to get rid of me!*

He felt heat rise through his flanks. His breath came quicker, and his ears tingled with anger. The surrounding dogs crowded around them. Alpha's posturing could not work this time. Surely everyone saw the way their "leader" had fallen apart in the face of the black cloud. Despite his deadly fangs and smooth words, the half wolf was a coward. He had no clue what to do in the face of disaster, no idea how to survive. Left to him, the dogs would have stayed at the old camp as the poisoned cloud drew closer. They would not have run when it made to pounce. All of them would have—

"For the sake of the Pack," barked Alpha again, "the City Dog must leave."

"If it weren't for me, none of you would have made it out of the forest alive," snapped Lucky, trying to control his rage. "*I* found the route away from the old camp. *I* led the way up the hill. The so-called 'Sky-Dog' you saw was a poison cloud, and the sight of it almost scared the fur off you, Alpha! You did nothing to help your Pack escape."

Alpha turned at him, snarling. "Face it, traitor: you're nothing but trouble. Your name is just a cruel joke. You and your bad luck aren't wanted here."

Daisy whimpered and ran to Lucky's side.

Big, gentle Martha took a step forward. "Lucky's a good friend to us," she said. "He always worked hard for the Leashed Dogs. He's never let us down."

"He pulled his weight in our Pack too," good-natured Snap put in. "He helped the smaller dogs climb the hill and led the way through the forest."

Whine yelped at this. "Snap's right; we should be grateful to Omega." The stout little dog nervously pawed the ground in a show of deference. It was obviously taking courage for him to speak out against the fearsome half wolf. "We wouldn't have made it without his help. Please reconsider, Alpha."

Lucky sighed. Whine had never spared him a kind word before, and he doubted that the little dog had had a change of heart now. He was probably just worried that with Lucky gone, he would go back to the rank he had cheated and blackmailed his way out of before the battle with the foxes.

The rank of Omega.

Alpha snarled at Whine, who scampered away with a whimper.

Then the dog-wolf flashed his teeth at Snap and Martha, who quickly dipped their heads in submission.

Lucky watched in disbelief. *They're following him, despite everything! They're going to let him kick me out of the Pack!*

Alpha took a step forward, puffed up to his full height. He stood over Lucky with his lips curled back in a snarl. "Need I remind you that your punishment remains outstanding, traitor?"

Lucky glared back at him but didn't speak. He was so angry that he didn't trust his voice. They were going to let their protests be pushed aside just like that, after all he'd done for them.

Alpha turned to the rest of his Pack, his voice soft and reasonable. "Considering the ordeal that we have been through, and the fact that Omega acted with *some* degree of bravery when we left our old camp, I would be prepared to spare him the wounds he deserves, and let him off with simple exile."

"Alpha's right. Omega would be better off if he just left." It was Sweet. She looked at Lucky with her big brown eyes and he sensed her hurt. He blinked back at her, sorry that he had let her down. Could she ever forgive him? And what good would her forgiveness do if he never saw her again? But something in his face must have angered Sweet, and she pulled back her lips. "You betrayed both Packs." The iciness of her snarl shocked Lucky. "How can any dog expect to be trusted after such dishonesty?"

Lucky flinched, no longer able to meet Sweet's eye. He turned to Bella instead. It had been her idea to spy on the Wild Pack in the first place—Lucky had just carried it out, thinking he would be finding a way for them all to share prey and territory together. He hadn't even wanted to do it—but his littermate had insisted it would help the Leashed Dogs.

Bella looked at him with a blank expression. She said nothing.

"Bella?" he yelped, and she dropped her gaze. What was she doing?

The other dogs stood by, staring at their paws. Even little Daisy would not look at Lucky, though she whimpered by his side.

They're all going to fall into line with Alpha . . . even the Leashed Dogs!

Their abandonment stung Lucky deeply. He would have expected some loyalty from these dogs, after everything they'd been through together. But there was none.

He exchanged a quick glance with Bella. She looked sad, but stern. Then he turned from the dogs without a word, scrambled up the rocks, and began to retrace his way to the forest.

He might discover a road, or another field. He would chase rabbits, drink from streams, find somewhere warm and dry to sleep.

I'll be free again, he told himself, willing his tail to wag. Instead it drooped behind him.

Freedom was all I ever wanted.

He had thought such things before and meant them, but now the words echoed through his mind. Had he become a dog who yearned for the same things the Leashed Dogs did—company and friendship . . . a Pack?

No, he told himself. *This is how it was* always *meant to be—me, by myself, without a Pack to slow me down. A true Lone Dog.*

With a whimper, Lucky climbed the path to the high trees, knowing those thoughts didn't ring true anymore.

He was not a Lone Dog now. Not really.

He was an outcast.

CHAPTER FIVE

It was sun-high before Lucky reentered the forest. Tall trees loomed overhead, the breeze fanning their branches. There was a gentle rise to the land as the forest climbed beyond the bank of the lake. He could hear the patter of paws in the undergrowth, and birds chirping above him. His stomach churned with hunger. He knew he could never catch a bird. The small animals that lived on the forest floor would also be too quick for him, invisible through the camouflage of leaves and vines. He would have to wait until he was out in the open air with a chance of gathering some speed.

Forest-Dog, please send me the cunning to find something to eat, and the wisdom to find a safe passage to . . .

Lucky gave a whine as he asked himself: *A safe passage to where? I have nowhere to go.*

He had run away from the other dogs without really thinking of where he was headed. He had tried to tell himself that he was meant to be a Lone Dog—but now he realized that being a Lone Dog in the forest was *nothing* like being a Lone Dog in the city. In the city, a Lone Dog had choices—there were always places to shelter, and the longpaws never stopped filling metal boxes with their discarded food. Here in the forest, things were very different. The only shelter was trees, and there were no food-boxes anywhere.

In the city, a Lone Dog could wander in circles and survive— but that wasn't possible in the forest. Lucky's fur prickled with rage and dread as he realized he had nowhere to go.

He plunged deeper into the forest, padding between the trees and catching the scent and sound of water. He used his head to clear a gap in some undergrowth and emerged at the bank of the river that the Leashed Pack had crossed to get to the Wild Pack's territory. Taking a step closer, Lucky breathed in the damp air. It was sweet and earthy and he detected none of the slimy green sludge that had made Bruno sick. He gazed at the river, briefly tapping it with his nose. It was cool and clear. Silver fish darted deep within the current, tempting but out of reach.

Satisfied that the water was clean, Lucky lapped at it thirstily. Once he had drunk his fill, he sat at the side of the bank and licked his paws, thinking things through.

Mickey had been sure that the longpaws were back. If he was

right that meant Lucky would be able to forage for food as he used to. No more chasing rabbits in long grass!

Lucky knew how to live in the city. If he hurried, he might even catch up with Mickey. This thought cheered him and he focused on his next move. One way to the city was over the hill, through the Wild Pack's old camp. But that would lead him along a path that ran right beneath the dark cloud. He didn't like to think of it still up there in the sky. It was hidden behind the trees now, but he could still smell that scent that singed his whiskers and prickled his nose.

Another route to the city was across the river. Lucky watched as the water darted through rocks, spinning in pelts of white froth. He thought of Martha and her affinity with the River-Dog. His chest tightened and his tail drooped—he wished that she were here with him. He missed her, and the others in the Pack. He whimpered at the thought of them, the sound seeming to bounce through the forest, from tree to tree.

How could they betray me, after all we've been through?

Pushing away his loneliness, Lucky rose and approached the river, sinking a single paw into the current. Its force immediately pulled him off-balance. He wrenched his paw away and stepped back. There was no way he could safely get across here.

He would have to find a way around it.

Lucky remembered that the Leashed Dogs had managed to cross upstream. He started following the path of the river, searching for the point where the current was more peaceful and the water shallow. He felt better now that he had quenched his thirst, but hunger still clawed at his belly.

A fly buzzed around his whiskers and he resisted the urge to snap his jaws in its direction. Things weren't *that* bad. He lowered his muzzle and ran his nose through a pile of leaves that had fallen to the forest floor. He picked up a couple between his teeth and chewed on them. Their sharp taste stung the back of his throat and would do nothing for his hunger in the long run, but at least they took his mind off it.

The screech of a crow made Lucky jump, his head darting toward the sky as he remembered the no-sun crow that had haunted him at the Wild Dog camp. Shimmering feathers vanished above the branches, but Lucky's gaze was drawn to something else in the sky. The poison cloud was drifting nearer, glistening like a puddle of black blood. He caught a whiff of its acrid stench. It was like something he had smelled in the city. It came back to him now—it was a loudcage scent, like the odor that rose from an injured loudcage as it bled onto the ground when they had their fierce fights.

Fights just like the ones that made black clouds rise into the air. The smell turned his stomach. There was nothing *natural* about it. But it couldn't be a loudcage fight—it was far too huge for that.

The cloud seemed to be drawing closer. Lucky's hackles rose and a growl escaped his throat, but he tore his gaze away and continued through the forest. The sooner he was out in the open, the sooner he could get away from the strange cloud. He lowered his muzzle and sniffed the earth, keen to dislodge the acrid smell. Inhaling the fragrance of damp leaves, moss, and grass, he began to relax.

Then he caught the scent of something unexpected—another dog!

Lucky froze, breathing deeply. The odor was familiar.

Twitch!

Lucky followed the scent-trail, his ears pricked and his tail straight behind him. After a little while, Lucky peered through a screen of lumbering vines and overgrown grass, and spotted Twitch in the distance. The injured dog was limping with deliberate, dragging steps between the trees. He disappeared behind a thick trunk, emerging on the other side to continue his slow progress.

Lucky felt a shudder of pity in his belly. The poor dog had

left the Pack before Lucky. He should have covered twice as much ground by now, but surely needed long rests in order to build up his strength to keep going. Maybe there were times when the pain in his leg became so great, he just had to stop. At this pace, he would be stuck in the forest at least another day.

Where is he heading?

Peering between two shrubs, Lucky watched the floppy-eared dog. He thought of barking to announce himself. But what if Twitch was angry at having been found? He'd left in the night, while the Pack was sleeping—surely he wanted to be alone?

Doubt gnawed at Lucky. He knew that dogs in pain could be highly dangerous. But Twitch was frail; he needed help. Warily Lucky started trailing the chase-dog, careful not to get too close. He watched as Twitch limped over fallen leaves before coming to a dead stop.

Lucky paused. *He must have picked up my scent.* He waited but Twitch stayed still, and it was impossible to read his mood at this distance.

Maybe it's better if I approach him side-on. From behind, it might feel like a challenge.

Lucky trod a wide arc between the trees, along Twitch's left. The injured dog moved a few paces to the right, taking a defensive stance. A low, unfriendly growl rumbled in his chest.

He obviously wants to be left alone. Didn't Twitch understand that the wild world was no place for a dog with a damaged leg? That he had almost no hope of surviving without some dog to watch his tail?

Lucky took another step forward, but Twitch shook his head and turned away, vanishing into the forest as quickly as his injured leg would take him. Lucky thought about following, but what could he do? He couldn't force Twitch to come with him. If this was his decision, Lucky had to respect it, even if it meant Twitch's death.

Lucky's tail drooped despondently as he turned away, resuming his path through the forest. Twitch's scent was soon lost beyond the smells of foliage and small creatures.

A wind rose through the trees, making branches shudder and leaves rustle. The Sun-Dog had moved across the sky and left a deeper shade of blue in his wake. White clouds hung long and the air felt damp. Coursing between them, the black cloud was like a dark lake hanging in the sky. Lucky's tail wound around his flank as he gave a whimper.

Forest-Dog, I know you're here, watching me as you watch over everything in the forest. Please keep me safe as the Sun-Dog moves toward his rest.

As he peered into the darkening sky, Lucky felt a drop of water tap his nose, and another blur in his eye before he blinked it away. He hurried beneath the trees, seeking shelter under a large tree with a broad trunk and a web of bulging roots that looked like snakes burrowing into the soil. Huddling among them, Lucky made himself as comfortable as he could.

The rain started coming more quickly, sheets of water escaping between the branches and tapping down from leaves. Lucky licked his sodden paws. *How has life come to this?* he thought miserably. He gave a long, lonely whine and lowered his head to ground.

A large raindrop hit Lucky's forehead above his eyes. Unlike the others, this one seemed to stay where it had fallen. Lucky felt a warm, tingling sensation creeping through all the way to his skin. He barked, shaking his fur to chase away the strange feeling of heat. He pawed at his head and looked up in time to see a dark flake fall on a raised root. It settled there, heavy and damp, the air above it twisting with steam. It was like black snow, the same color as the dark cloud.

Lucky watched as more flakes tumbled onto the mulch of the forest floor. Beneath the flakes, the grass seemed to wilt and bow. Lucky rose to his paws, his heart thumping in his chest.

Black snow, falling from the sky! What's going on?

He became aware of a powerful burning stench, like an invisible fire racing up his nose and making his eyes fill with water. It seemed to be coming from every tree in the forest. The heavy rain must have masked it at first, but now Lucky knew what it was.

The scent of the dark cloud was descending on him like a deadly enemy.

It wasn't water that fell from the mysterious cloud, but curious black flakes that drooled a rancid steam. Lucky scampered to avoid them as they fluttered to the ground, throwing himself beneath branches. He yelped as he shook himself, wishing he were out in the open.

The black flakes did not drop evenly, the way rain did. They fell in hot clumps, spinning and tangling with branches, smoldering against the forest floor.

Lucky yelped in horror. *The black cloud is falling to earth!*

Swarms of ash slowly tumbled to the ground. It looked like the kind of dark, dirty clouds that longpaws made when cooking food outside on open fires. The food had smelled delicious, but there had been something *wrong* about the fires—the smoke's odor was sharp and unnatural.

Had fire caused *this* black cloud?

Lucky gaped at the tumbling black flakes. Such a fire would

have to have been unimaginably huge. Where *was* it? Where was the black cloud coming from?

He remembered Mickey's conviction that the cloud was the shape of a longpaw, pointing the way for dogs to travel. Alpha had been just as sure that it had taken the form of an angry Sky-Dog. Now Lucky was certain that they were both wrong.

The black cloud had to be linked to the Big Growl. It had to be connected to the crumbling earth, the shattering skies, the poisonous water and bad smells. If it was a sign of anything, it was that nothing had improved: The world since the Growl was just as dangerous as ever.

Then the realization dawned on him. *The longpaws have not returned. The city will be just as we left it. Deserted.*

He thought of Mickey, wide-eyed and hopeful, still carrying his longpaw's glove in his jaws. Had he reached the city yet? What would he do when he got there? Would Mickey try to enter his longpaw's den, as Alfie had? He could get killed among the poisonous fumes and collapsing walls. Even if he stayed safe, how would he survive? There would be no food to eat and no clean water to drink. And what of the animals and longpaws who'd died there, with no one to bury them? Lucky shuddered.

Poor Mickey, carrying that glove, keeping it safe. So loyal to his longpaw. He'd been a good friend to the Leashed Dogs too, and had always stood by Lucky. He was not responsible for Lucky's exile. He didn't even know about it. . . .

I can't leave him to face all that alone.

Lucky bounded out from beneath the trees, swerving this way and that to avoid the black flakes. He ran as fast as he could, his paws splattering against the wet forest floor. Brown streaks of mud caked his flanks, and his fur was soon soaked through with rain, but he barked excitedly. He had a mission now, a reason to leave the forest, to reach the city. He had *somewhere* to go.

He had to find Mickey as soon as he could.

CHAPTER SIX

Lucky swallowed down the last of the rabbit and yawned luxuriously. His full belly sighed with gratitude and he offered his thanks. *Forest-Dog, you always watch over me. The rabbit was delicious.*

He hadn't expected to catch anything until he was out in open fields, but he'd found a small clearing between the trees and there it had been, gazing up at the sky. Perhaps he had the dark cloud to thank for that.

Lucky licked his lips, reminding himself that he couldn't depend on trapping a rabbit again. And he had to admit that it was harder to hunt alone, particularly where tree trunks and branches concealed the path. Small animals had so many places to hide.

At least it had stopped raining. The black cloud had dispersed into smaller clumps of floating ash that loomed overhead in dark clots. Lucky couldn't wait to get out of the forest.

He pressed on between the trees, pushing uphill as the light started fading and the Sun-Dog padded across the sky. Eventually the land flattened out. Lucky knew he should be pleased at this—flatter terrain surely meant that he was drawing nearer to the city, where he would find Mickey.

Yet a prickle of unease touched the fur of his neck. He felt like he knew this place, but he could not remember exactly how or why. The acrid remnants of the ash smothered his senses and memories. He tried to ignore the shiver that ran along his back. He would just have to hurry, to keep on moving, even after the Sun-Dog had gone to sleep. He journeyed toward the river, springing over a fallen trunk.

Ahead of him was a huge mound of black ash, the sharp smell instantly catching his nose. With a yelp, Lucky turned to get away from it. His paws skidded on fallen leaves, and he smacked against a long, low branch that swung into the towering ash. Dislodged, it started sliding to the ground in clumps, creating an avalanche of foul smells and black snow.

Lucky turned and scrambled in the opposite direction. He would have to find another path across the river.

He climbed a hill, his fur rising again. His tail stiffened and his ears pricked up instinctively. He felt as though he could *almost* smell something. Something familiar. Something dangerous . . .

He cursed the black flakes for masking all other scents beneath their powerful stench. Creeping farther up the slope, Lucky's location struck him. In a rush of smells, of sight and memories, he recognized the hill and the valley below. Fear shuddered along his spine. He was very close to the Fierce Dogs' lair, he realized—much closer than he would have liked. He remembered the brutal army of dogs with their thick, muscular bodies, their pointed ears, and their shiny black coats. He had hidden from them in their eerie Dog-Garden, watching them patrol their territory, and though he had outwitted the Fierce Dogs and escaped, he never wanted to face those dogs again. A tremor of panic ran through his belly and Lucky froze.

In the distance he heard barking, deep and foreboding. He lowered his muzzle and sniffed, trying to blank out the foul ash. Then he caught it: the tang of blood.

It took everything he had to ignore the impulse to run away. He needed to find out what was happening here. He couldn't just run. Lucky threw a cautious look over his back. What if the Fierce Dogs had found the hole in the fence that had allowed him to escape? What if they ran patrols around their territory as far as the forested hills? Were some of them out there now in the gloom, watching him?

A piercing howl broke from the valley below and Lucky whined with fright. Careful to stay upwind, Lucky stalked closer to the Fierce Dogs' lair, hoping that the smell of ash would conceal his approach.

It took a few minutes to reach the wall of the Dog-Garden and in that time the noises had hushed. Then he heard it again, much closer, on the far side of the wall. They were the desperate howls of a dog in pain, whimpering, begging for mercy. Lucky knew that he should keep his distance—how dangerous would a *wounded* Fierce Dog be?

Lucky crept along the wall, his ears pricked. He picked up the smell of other dogs in the yard. Those dogs surely knew about their Packmate. They either didn't care, or had intended the dog to be harmed. Either way, they would hardly take kindly to Lucky's appearance.

A twig snapped and Lucky caught the shadow of a Fierce Dog several long-strides away. A huge, stocky male, with a thick neck and a pointed snout, it sniffed at the ground and cast its head left and right.

It's outside the fence! So the Fierce Dogs had found a way through after all. Was this Fierce Dog looking for prey, or intruders?

Lucky held his breath. *Run! Before he sees you and raises the alarm!*

There was nothing to be done for the wounded dog, he told himself firmly. He backed away as silently as he could and retraced his steps through the forest, careful not to crunch any leaves beneath his paws on his ascent. Only a foolish dog would hang around and wait to be discovered. If they caught his scent, the Fierce Dogs would surely rip him apart.

Keep running to the city. It's Mickey you should be helping. He's the one whose life can still be saved.

Another yelp of anguish rose from the Fierce Dogs' lair. As Lucky hurried back up the hill toward the city, he felt a pang of guilt. A vague memory returned to him from puppyhood. His Mother-Dog had been talking about the difference between wolves and dogs. Wolves were cunning and sneaky. Dogs were noble. Dogs did not leave another dog to die.

I'm sorry, Forest-Dog. I want to help but I can't. . . . Please look after the Fierce Dog.

He'd never expected the world to bring him to this.

Lucky shook his fur vigorously. He'd walked through no-sun and had crossed the river at its shallowest point. The River-Dog had eased the soreness in his neck and leg where the foxes had bitten him, washing away the pain with firm strokes of his icy tongue.

The cool water had shocked Lucky's tired muscles and given him new energy and strength. He did not want to stop now—he had to keep going until he reached the city. Mickey might be there already. Lucky pictured him slowly starving to death but refusing to leave, waiting for longpaws who would never return.

The journey had been tiring, full of dips and inclines where the tall trees clung to the ground. Finally Lucky reached the highest point in the forest. He stopped and looked around. The Sun-Dog trod his path over the land, casting a gentle morning light. White clouds twisted in the sky and the air was damp and clean.

Almost hidden in the distance beyond the soft borders of treetops was the shimmering lake. The nearer end of the lake was in the Wild Pack's abandoned territory. On its far side, by a collection of craggy rocks, were the friends he had left behind. He thought of Bella, his litter-sister, and the other Leashed Dogs. He wondered how they were faring in the larger Pack, and hoped that Alpha wasn't being too hard on them. Then he pictured Sweet with her large dark eyes. His belly clenched as he thought of her, remembering that look of betrayal. . . .

He turned toward a clearing with rolling fields below. It was the Leashed Dogs' first territory, where they had learned to hunt and work as a team. He felt a surge of pride in his friends, despite everything—they had come a long way since they had first left the city.

With renewed energy, Lucky ran, dashing through the trees to open fields of grass until he could see jagged outlines of long-paw homes rise up against the skyline. They grew up like weeds around him as he stepped from the soft, muddy grass back onto the hard, cracked surface of the streets.

Lucky slowed his pace as he entered the city, sniffing for signs of bad air, listening for the familiar rumble of loudcages. But there was only silence. The loudcages stood lifeless between pools of shattered clear-stone. Beneath their twisted muzzles were dried pools of the juice longpaws fed them.

The loudcages have been bleeding.

The roads were cracked and Lucky had to leap over a foul-smelling stream. The water glistened, its oily sheen catching the light of the Sun-Dog, which climbed overhead.

The city was still deserted. The longpaws had not returned.

It was odd to be back here, to feel the hard stone under his paws. To his surprise, Lucky realized he had become used to the feel of grass. He felt a sudden longing for his old life of wandering, scavenging food, and relaxing with his friends, never depending on anyone else. But there was no denying that part of his life had gone, perhaps for good.

The city he had left behind had not returned to normal. He could never live here again.

Lucky slunk through the quiet streets, searching for the Leashed Dogs' homes. The buildings looked familiar, though changed. The grass in front of the houses had grown almost as tall as he was, and vines crept along the walls without the longpaws to contain them. Everything looked tired and deserted.

He reached the corner of the street where the Leashed Dogs had lived before the Big Growl. Like the other buildings, the houses looked bent, their yards overgrown with neglect. Lucky watched from a distance, sniffing the air, wondering where Mickey had gone. He expected his friend to greet him with excited yaps, but the Farm Dog was nowhere to be seen.

If he isn't here, where is he?

Lucky's heart sank. What should he do now? Explore the city? No, there was nothing for him here anymore. Not even the scraps of food he'd once scavenged.

Lucky shook himself, took a deep breath, and sniffed again. *Mickey!* Yes, he was certain: His friend was nearby. *But why can't I see him?*

Lucky followed his nose over the cracked ground, his whiskers tingling; at last, he saw a flash of black-and-white fur in the shadow of a loudcage. Mickey was crouched there. Something in the Farm Dog's scent and posture made Lucky uneasy, and he kept low as he approached, making sure he did not seem threatening.

"Mickey? It's me, Lucky. I've been looking for you."

Mickey gave a flick of the ear but he kept his eyes fixed, staring across the street beyond Lucky.

Lucky paused. "What's wrong? What are you hiding from?"

"I'm not hiding!" Mickey growled. "I'm *waiting*. Look."

Lucky followed his gaze. At the far end of the street he saw movement—two longpaws clambering out of a house near the corner of the street.

Unlike the ones he had seen in the fields beyond the city, these longpaws did not have black, mouthless faces and bright yellow fur. Instead they had pelts like the old longpaws used to, but they were torn and the skin underneath was filthy. He watched as they dragged out a large, flat object made of dried tree that had four pawless legs.

Some instinct made Lucky draw back behind the loudcages. These longpaws reminded Lucky of the ones he had seen sometimes before the Big Growl, when he used to roam the streets.

Unlike most longpaws, this type did not seem to live in Packs. They lived outside, huddling in their shaggy, dirty pelts. They stank of fire-juice, and would yelp and squabble among themselves constantly, and when they approached other longpaws, they would be chased away.

But now there were no other longpaws to be seen.

Lucky and Mickey watched as the shabby-furred longpaws removed more objects from the house and piled them in the high grass. They dropped them heavily, one of the longpaws leaning over to spit on the pavement. Even from this distance, Lucky could see that the pool of saliva was yellow and there was yellow froth around the longpaw's muzzle. His face was gaunt and sallow, and Lucky spotted the bones jutting out at the base of his neck. Lucky knew that hunger made longpaws crazy, and this was the hungriest longpaw he had ever seen.

The dogs would have to keep their distance.

The longpaws were on the move, pushing open the door to the next house and stumbling inside. Lucky could hear dragging and crashing sounds.

Mickey snarled beneath his breath, his haunches low and ears pressed flat as he watched in silence. "Nasty, disgusting longpaws," he growled, shifting slightly, still crouching by the loudcage.

"They'd better not go near *my* longpaws' house. They better not even think about it!"

Lucky was not entirely sure *what* the longpaws were thinking about. There couldn't be any food for them to find—not after all this time. He kept a wary eye on Mickey as the longpaws advanced, disappearing into each house and reappearing with things they had found inside.

They were getting closer and closer to Mickey's old home.

They seemed more... *wild* than ordinary longpaws. He thought about the Leashed Dogs and how they had struggled. Those who didn't learn to survive in this strange new world would surely have starved to death. It must have been the same for the longpaws who were left behind, forgotten by those who had fled the city, just as the Leashed Dogs had been abandoned by their masters.

Mickey stood up straight, his back legs stiffening. He watched with a low growl as the longpaws stopped in front of his old home. They yapped loudly at each other, one bending forward and coughing as the other leaned against the wall.

"Mickey, it's not safe," Lucky said in a soft voice. "Those long-paws are dangerous. You don't know what they might do."

Mickey turned around sharply. "I have a duty to my long-paws' home." His ears twitched and he narrowed his eyes. "You wouldn't understand. You were a Lone Dog before the Big Growl. What are you doing here, anyway? I thought you were one of the Pack these days."

Lucky was stung, but he pressed on. "Your longpaws left a long time ago!"

"It's still their home," Mickey growled. "*Mine,* too. All my life I've been brought up to defend it. I have to stop these scavengers!" He turned to the longpaws and barked furiously, his ears pressed against his head. Lucky cringed, but the longpaws ignored Mickey and stood yapping in front of the house.

One of the longpaws kicked the door open and both of them disappeared inside. Mickey threw a desperate look at Lucky.

Lucky could see how much this meant to his friend. "Okay . . . follow me, and do what I do," he instructed. He pulled back his lips, revealing his teeth. Mickey did the same. Growling, he entered the doorway as the longpaws crossed between rooms. One of them glanced at him, but they didn't stop what they were doing.

Mickey started to bark again. "They're ignoring us! We should charge at them!"

"Trust me," urged Lucky. He remembered a small, wiry-haired dog with a pointy nose who he'd known in the city before the Big

Growl. The little dog used to terrify passing longpaws, despite his size. He did it not by barking and hopping around but by standing perfectly still and growling. The trick was to look confident.

Longpaws don't know what a dog is thinking. And that scares them.

Mickey took his cue, doing a good impression of Lucky, lips curled back and snarling steadily. The two dogs edged deeper into the house, approaching a small room where both longpaws were busy gathering objects. The dogs stood at the entrance, almost motionless, growling in low voices.

The longpaws looked again at the dogs, and stopped moving around. One threw his hands in the air and started barking at the dogs. Lucky held his ground and Mickey did the same, paws planted to the floor and growling all the time.

The longpaws yelped to each other. Up close, Lucky could see the yellow spit gathering at their mouths. Their lips had a green tinge, which reminded Lucky of the poisonous river-water that had made Bruno sick. The one that had tried to shoo them away had angry pink scabs along his jawline. He took a step back but the other longpaw made a grab for a deep, clear-stone dish, and waved it in front of Lucky. The hairs prickled along Lucky's back and fear coursed through him, his paw pads suddenly damp with sweat. Despite this, he held firm. The longpaw flung the object and it flew past Lucky's head, smashing against the wall. Lucky flinched but continued to growl, and Mickey only snarled louder.

Lucky's ears flipped back at the sound of a deep groan. The house was speaking! His body tensed. Was it moving? Would it collapse?

The longpaw who had hurled the clear-stone hastily gathered up more objects to throw at the dogs. Lucky sensed Mickey stiffen, preparing for an onslaught, but the Farm Dog didn't even whimper when a heavy object clipped his ear. Lucky was impressed.

"You're doing great!" he told Mickey. "You've got them spooked!"

There was a twitch of pleasure in his friend's tail as he held his stance and continued to snarl.

Lucky could see the longpaws exchanging nervous glances, backing against the wall of the small room. Then the house growled loudly and a shower of dust fell from above them. One of the longpaws started coughing and Lucky barked at them:

"Get out of here! This is not your place! Get out before we make you!"

His bark echoed back at him in the small room and seemed to dislodge more dust, which fell in white shrouds.

The longpaws cowered, backs against the wall. Lucky felt a

wave of satisfaction when he caught the scent of their fear. He knew that they would not defend themselves against an attack—they would run away at the first opportunity. He turned to bark to Mickey but the ground shuddered beneath their paws as the house growled again. With a whine, a long wound tore open along one wall, crawling upward and bleeding more dust and debris.

The longpaws yelped fearfully, dropping the objects they had gathered and shoving each other out of the way as they made for the door. They hurried past the dogs, coughing as they broke into the open.

Lucky nudged Mickey urgently. "We have to get out!" he barked.

Mickey's eyes were wild, shooting around the room.

"But my longpaws—"

"Now!" snarled Lucky.

With an ear-piercing *crack*, the side of the room started sinking and the ceiling rocked.

The house! thought Lucky. *It's falling down!*

CHAPTER SEVEN

Lucky and Mickey scrambled outside and bolted across the road to a stretch of grass in front of another longpaw house. They spun around in time to see a wall of Mickey's old home buckle. Its guts sprayed through cracks and rained on the front lawn. There was the sound of tearing and cracking. The buckling wall folded inward, crushing whatever remained inside. Mickey walked a tight circle, trembling and yelping in despair.

Lucky caught his friend's wild expression. "No!" he barked. "Stay back! Your longpaws are far away."

Mickey dropped to the ground, his flanks heaving. "I know," he whined. "But . . . I *must* defend the house!"

Lucky licked his friend's nose. "There's nothing to defend," he soothed. "Your longpaws left long ago."

There was another crack and the front door bulged forward.

Debris from the broken building poured out of it, blocking the path.

"You would have been killed if you had stayed there a moment longer. Both of us would have been."

Mickey yelped in acknowledgment. Both dogs crouched low to the grass, panting. The noises had died down. Now there was only the occasional clunk or crash and billows of white mist around the building.

Without warning, Mickey sprang to his paws, throwing back his head and howling: "All the good longpaws have gone! They've gone! Only the bad ones are left!"

Mickey walked a few paces and howled again, now addressing his departed longpaws. "Why did you leave me? I would never have left *you*! Why did you go?"

Lucky stayed quiet. *Let him get it out,* he thought.

Mickey's howls grew louder. "You let me come upstairs, you gave me treats. . . . You took me to the big garden, we played together. . . . I waited for you when I was alone in the house. . . . I thought about you all the time. Why didn't you take me with you?"

Eventually the black-and-white dog fell silent. He flopped

back onto the grass and dropped his head, his eyes still fixed on the house.

"I thought they'd come back," he whimpered. His ears twitched. "The other longpaws, the bad ones . . . we challenged them, we scared them with our growls and teeth. I could smell their fear-scent. That's not how it used to be. I've never threatened longpaws before."

"The world has changed since the Big Growl," said Lucky.

"That's the thing. It wasn't only the earth that was scarred and altered," whined Mickey miserably. "It has changed the dogs who walk on it." He sniffed the ground. "Earth-Dog, what happened to you?" He pawed the ground a moment and sighed, turning his shining, dark eyes to Lucky. "I was wrong to leave the Pack and come back here. I realize now that we have nothing left but each other." Mickey tilted his head. "Lucky, I'm sorry I was so unfriendly when you arrived. It was those horrible longpaws, and you took me by surprise, that's all. I'm glad to see you but . . . why are you here? Did you leave the Pack too?"

Lucky looked away, beyond his friend, to the dust that still swirled around the broken home.

"I *had* to go, Mickey." He shivered when he remembered how

Alpha had thrown him out. None of the dogs had stood their ground against the half wolf, not even the Leashed Dogs. He didn't want to talk about that now.

"I know, I know, you're a 'Lone Dog,'" Mickey barked. "But you relied on longpaws as much as we did. With them all gone, maybe there's no place for Lone Dogs anymore? The Pack is our family now. We need to go back, Lucky. We need to tell them that we made a mistake."

Lucky swallowed, his throat dry. He was happy that Mickey was ready to leave this place of death and decay. Mickey would be safer in the Pack. But the dogs would never allow Lucky to come back. He felt a sad weight on his chest.

"You're right; this is no place for a dog anymore," he said. The city was poisoned. *Nothing* could live here for long.

Mickey was gazing at him, a twinkle in his brown eyes and his tail thumping the ground. "It's not that far, Lucky. We both made it in good time, didn't we? If we hurry, we could even be there by next no-sun." He rose to his paws, panting.

There was genuine cheerfulness in his face. Lucky couldn't remember the last time he had seen it. *He's so happy because he doesn't feel lost anymore. He's finally accepted that his longpaws have gone. I can't tell him now that the Pack forced me out, not yet.*

Lucky rose to his paws. "If you really want to go back . . . well, I'll come *some* of the way with you."

Mickey barked excitedly, licking Lucky's ears.

"I can't rejoin the Pack, though," Lucky added quickly.

Mickey started hopping and prancing back and forth. "Can't or won't? When will you stop pretending that you're better off on your own? You're safer and happier in the Pack; you know you are!" He nipped Lucky's ear playfully. "You *clearly* belong with other dogs. And the Pack needs you, as well. We've only survived this far with your help."

Lucky didn't answer this but gave Mickey a good-natured shove with his head, pleased to see his friend's spirits so high. He hadn't expected him to recover so quickly.

I've come all this way to keep him safe, Lucky thought. *I can't waste an opportunity to do just that.* "Let's go," he said, his tail starting to wag in spite of himself.

Mickey growled happily, nudging Lucky as the two dogs play-fought in the long grass. Then Lucky broke away and started bounding along the road, making toward the path out of the city.

"Wait!" Mickey barked.

Lucky turned, his ears pricked up. "Is something wrong?"

"No. There's just something I need to do. . . ."

Lucky watched as Mickey disappeared behind a loudcage, the one where he had first spotted the black-and-white dog watching his longpaws' house. A moment later, Mickey reappeared, the longpaw glove held in his jaws. It was worn and filthy, stuffing trailing from a tear in the fabric, but Mickey carried it as though it was the most precious thing on earth. His tail no longer wagging, he walked solemnly toward the house. Lucky was about to stop him when Mickey paused before the front lawn that was now dusted white.

He stood a few minutes in silence, gazing at the wrecked house. Then he trod carefully over the lawn, kicking up puffs of dust. He set down the glove on the broken front step where the door used to be. He gave it a tentative lick, cleansing it of dust and dirt. Then he took a step back.

The glove shone clean and fragile like a small creature amid the rubble. Mickey seemed to speak directly to it as he whined:

"I am going now. I have to leave you behind and go into the wild to live with the Pack. Everything has changed, and in this world without longpaws, dogs must make their own way."

Mickey glanced at Lucky, who lowered his muzzle respectfully. He didn't understand the way the Farm Dog felt. He had never shared a bond with a longpaw. But if it made Mickey so loyal that he would defend their house even after they'd abandoned him . . . well, maybe they weren't *all* bad.

Mickey continued. "If you ever come back, you will find this thing, your possession, which you gave to me. It was my favorite toy, and when I played with it, I thought of you. This will prove that I came back to look for you—that I never forgot you or stopped loving you."

Mickey turned away from the place he'd once called his home. Lucky felt certain he'd never lay eyes on it again.

Lucky led the way along the broad, leafy streets lined with sleeping loudcages. Mickey padded behind him. They stayed in the center of the street, keeping away from the leaning houses, which creaked and groaned. Lucky feared that they might collapse at any moment, just as Mickey's longpaws' house had. *We need to get out of here as quickly as possible,* he thought.

Ears pricked, he listened to the growls and groans of the buildings. He was surprised when he caught a distant rumbling sound, not from the streets or the ground, but from above him. His eyes shot up, searching for rain clouds. The sky was clear and blue, and the air was warm following the showers of the previous night. Even the black cloud had disappeared, its poison ash spewed in dark pools or clinging to trees in the forest. Still, there was a whirr and grumble in the air, and Lucky shot Mickey a worried look.

"Thunder!" barked Mickey, a fearful look crossing his face. "The Sky-Dogs are angry again!"

Lucky needed Mickey to keep calm. He turned to sniff the air. It was dry. "I don't think so. . . . " Lucky's hackles rose and his ears twisted, trying to understand the whirring sounds.

Mickey's tail froze. "What's that?"

Lucky spun around. High over the jagged horizon of buildings, he could now see something huge, as big as a loudcage, bobbing in the sky. Was it a bird? As he and Mickey watched, another one came into view, darting down lower and hovering above some houses, proceeding with jerky, angry swoops. Their huge wings spun over their heads in circles, slicing the air with a noise like thunder.

"I don't like it," Mickey whined. His eyes flicked wildly across the road. "We should get out of here."

"Hold on," said Lucky. As the birds looped overhead, they whipped up a wind that tore the leaves from trees and set the dogs' hairs on end. But Lucky yelped as he saw there was something even stranger about these huge birds. Their bodies were shiny and smooth and they both had deep holes in their flanks where their insides were exposed to the open air.

Lucky could see right *inside* their bellies!

He craned his neck. Something yellow was moving about in there. The color . . . he knew that color.

Longpaws!

Longpaws trapped inside the birds! It was such a strange sight that Lucky's eyes had struggled to understand what they were seeing. Now he was certain: Those hostile longpaws with their bright, shiny pelts were barking at one another as they shifted about in the birds' bellies.

Mickey must have spotted them at the same time. "Long-paws!" he yelped. "What's that one doing?"

A longpaw in the first bird was edging toward the hole in its shiny flank. He half climbed through, hanging outside in the open air. The bird seemed to help him by dipping to one side so that the longpaw was dangling toward the broken houses, point-ing and barking back to the others.

Lucky felt a tremble of uncertainty run through his body. "They're searching . . . I think."

"Searching for what?" Mickey asked.

There were three of them now—three huge birds, whirring,

their wings whipping up the air around them. One swooped closer, a longpaw still dangling from the wound in its flank. The others dispersed over the city. Lucky could just make out other yellow-furred longpaws pressing their faces against the see-through bellies.

The dogs cowered, their fur blown flat, blinking against the wind that stirred beneath the birds' wings. One bird stayed overhead, hovering and hunting. But what was it looking for?

Then all three birds veered sharply toward the city outskirts. They dropped lower as they disappeared from view.

"They're going to land in the forest!" Lucky barked over the receding thunder of their wings. "I think we should follow them and find out what they're up to!"

Mickey was reluctant. "What if they see us? The birds are carrying those horrible, yellow-furred longpaws. They're *dangerous*, Lucky."

"We'll keep a safe distance."

"Don't you remember how they shouted at us? How they kicked Daisy?"

Lucky did remember. He watched the silhouette of the huge birds whirring lower until he could no longer see them behind the buildings.

"We won't get close to the longpaws or those birds," he barked. "But it's no good ignoring them. We need to understand what they're searching for. We need to know if they're a threat. Maybe it will give us a clue to where the other longpaws have gone. It's a risk we have to take."

Mickey's eyes were wide and his black ears were low.

"If you're sure . . ."

Lucky watched the sky a moment longer, though he could no longer see the great birds in the distance. "We have to do this. We have to find out what they're up to!" He bolted along the road with Mickey close behind. Their paws pounded against the hard stone of the city streets as they raced back to the forest.

CHAPTER EIGHT

Thorns and long grass tugged against Lucky's belly as the dogs slunk low to the ground, weaving their way through the undergrowth. He could hear the thrumming of the huge birds but couldn't see them beyond the thick foliage.

"I'm not sure this is a good idea," whined Mickey.

Lucky was worn out from his long journey through no-sun and their escape from the collapsing longpaw house. He didn't have the energy to argue anymore. He shot Mickey a sharp look and the black-and-white dog lowered his head and followed obediently.

It was easy to locate the massive birds, even when they'd sunk below the tree line. They made so much noise that all the wildlife of the forest scurried away from them as quickly as it could.

Lucky led Mickey through a clutch of low hedges, following the path of a flock of starlings fleeing in terror. Emerging into a clearing, the dogs saw three metal birds settled on the grass. Their wings whipped up a gale that warped the branches of surrounding trees and unleashed a blizzard of leaves. Lucky and Mickey ducked low, squinting against wind and debris. Then the wings began to slow.

"What do you think is going on?" Mickey barked.

As the dogs watched, hunkered low behind the hedge, the frightening yellow-furred longpaws spilled from the birds' guts. They ran toward the forest, carrying strange, rigid sheets between them.

"They look a bit like longpaw beds," Mickey whined. "Except without the comfortable thick fur. What are they for?"

Lucky just shook his head. He had no idea.

The birds were resting, their wings turning lazily now as the air grew calmer around them. The high barks of longpaws cut through the air and Mickey yelped. The yellow-furred longpaws who had gone into the forest reappeared, carrying a third longpaw on the bed between them.

Even from this distance, Lucky could see that there was something wrong with him. He was twisted onto one side. Like the other longpaws, his pelt was vivid yellow, but unlike them his face was exposed. His mouth was frothing with yellow spit and his pale skin was waxy. Lucky could smell the metal tang of blood in the air.

"The longpaw is wounded," he told Mickey.

They looked on, concealed behind the hedge, as the longpaws hurried their injured Pack member to the first bird and slid him inside.

Mickey whined with fear. "That's horrible!" he yelped. "A beast big enough and fierce enough to eat longpaws whole! They caught a weak one and they're feeding him to the loudbird!"

"I'm not sure . . . it doesn't seem to hurt him." Lucky's tail twitched and the whiskers bristled at his muzzle. The yellow-furred longpaws were climbing into the bird's belly. *They are choosing to go back inside the beast,* Lucky thought. "I don't know what's going on," he admitted. "Maybe we should move on."

"Yes, let's." Mickey whined in relief.

Lucky continued to stare at the loudbird for a little longer. He wished he could understand what it was doing. Why were longpaws always such a mystery?

His ears pricked up and he spun around when he heard a loud rustling not six long-strides behind them. He saw a flash of shiny yellow.

"It's the longpaws!" he whimpered as quietly as he could, eager not to draw their attention. "The ones who came out of the other birds."

The longpaws were stalking through the tall grass, dipping down as though searching for something. They were drawing nearer.

Beside Lucky, Mickey pawed the ground, his eyes wild. "Let's get out of here," he begged.

Lucky gave a brief nod of his head. Keeping low to the ground, they slunk between the hedge and deeper into the forest. Lucky remembered that there were another couple of yellow-furred longpaws out there that they hadn't accounted for. They would need to be careful.

The two dogs trod warily through the dense foliage, stepping over stout bushes and pools of ivy. Once Lucky was satisfied that the yellow-furred longpaws were safely behind them, he started to pick up the pace. Keen to avoid the mounds of foul ash he had passed before, he cut a sharp path between the trees, taking a new direction while circling toward the calmer section of the river. He could already detect its damp, earthy scent. They would be able to cross there and put a good distance between themselves and these strange longpaws.

As they reached the bank of the river, the dreadful whirring of the loudbirds' wings began again. They were much farther away now, but they still whipped up a wind strong enough to pummel the branches of the trees. A moment later the birds rose to the sky, hovering over the forest threateningly before swooping back toward the city.

Mickey whimpered. "I wish we knew where they were going. And if they're coming back. . . ."

The dogs stood and watched until the loudbirds were dots on the horizon.

Mickey turned to Lucky as they continued their journey through the forest. "Since the Big Growl, everything I thought I knew has changed forever."

Lucky could only bark in acknowledgment. He was trying to make sense of what they'd just seen.

What were those huge loudbirds, and why did they land in the forest? The longpaws seemed to be looking for something. Lucky blinked back over his shoulder. *All those longpaws had that horrible yellow fur. It's as though they're from a single Pack. But it was so . . .* big. *Normally a longpaw Pack is small— four or five at most. Maybe even the longpaws have changed their Pack rules after the Big Growl.*

Lucky didn't know why, but the thought made his fur bristle nervously.

Mickey went on. "The good longpaws have gone and only the scary ones with yellow fur are left, or the ragged, mean ones that bark and spit." His ears drooped sadly. "None of us Leashed Dogs could have imagined Pack life before. Now it's the only thing that makes sense."

Lucky knew where the Farm Dog was going with this.

"I *left*, Mickey," he replied quietly. "I can't go back."

"Why not?" Mickey whined. "I left too. If we reason with Bella . . ."

"It isn't Bella we need to worry about." Lucky suppressed a growl, thinking of Alpha. As much as Lucky wanted to confront the arrogant dog-wolf, he knew that he didn't stand a chance against him in open combat. Alpha might be a coward in the face of the unknown, but he knew how to fight and kill.

"Alpha will forgive us for leaving," Mickey countered. "We're both good hunters. Or we can patrol. You have the best nose of any dog . . . and . . ." Mickey paused. "Don't you *miss* everyone?"

Lucky turned back to the path, where a fallen tree trunk blocked the way. He considered the two Packs who'd joined forces. There were plenty among them who he missed, and his tail sank at the thought.

"You can go back, Mickey. Alpha will let you. Not me. . . ."

The black-and-white dog barked in frustration. "You're so stubborn, Lucky! When will you admit that you aren't a Lone Dog anymore? You're a Pack dog; we all are. You need us and we need you!"

Why don't I just tell him that I was cast out by Alpha? That nobody spoke up for me, or tried to change his mind?

But Lucky couldn't bring himself to say the words. His tail lowered and shame crept over him. He didn't want the Farm Dog to know that the other dogs had turned on him.

Mickey's my friend, Lucky told himself. *He won't judge me. He'll understand if I explain what happened.*

He lifted his head to tell Mickey his story when he caught a sharp new scent.

Fur . . . and skin.

Another dog!

Lucky stiffened, his hackles rising. Was it Twitch? Perhaps he could be persuaded to rejoin the Pack too. He could travel with Lucky and Mickey. . . . But the breeze carried the scent away. Maybe it was an old, stale scent, still lingering.

"Why did you stop? Did you smell something?" Mickey asked.

"No," Lucky barked, leaping over the fallen trunk and bounding the rest of the way to the riverbank. "I guess I didn't."

* * *

They were panting when they reached the river. It sparkled, silvery beneath the light of the Sun-Dog. The water was still fresh and clean here, and Lucky and Mickey drank happily.

Mickey yipped. "That's the tastiest water I've ever had! The best, the best!" He pounced on Lucky and they rolled on the leafy earth. It was a relief for Lucky to feel his spirits lighten. For a few moments, he didn't want to think about anything—not the city, nor the strange loudbirds they'd encountered. Mickey nipped Lucky amiably on the neck. "Urgh! You're covered in dirt!"

Lucky spun around and pinned Mickey down with his front paws.

"Is that so?" he yapped. "Are you surprised after all that dust from the longpaw house? You think you're any cleaner?"

He leaned forward as though to nip Mickey, but instead he licked his friend's muzzle. "What we really need is a proper wash! I hope you're ready to do more than just drink this river-water."

Mickey leaped to his paws. "More than ready!" he howled.

Please, River-Dog, thought Lucky. *Carry us safely to the other side.* He plunged in, feeling the mud and grime fall from his fur. He kicked his paws beneath him, neck craned as he cut across the current, thrilled by the cool water. Mickey swam alongside him, panting happily.

They climbed out onto the sun-soaked bank of the river, catching their breath. Lucky shook himself vigorously. He couldn't remember when he'd last felt so clean. Mickey started shaking himself too, and as water sprayed in Lucky's eyes he barked and pawed the ground. The cool water had removed not only the dirt that had clung to their fur, but any last traces of tiredness. Lucky butted his friend's neck, ready to prance and run through the forest. He felt light and free for the first time since he'd been exiled from the Pack.

The two dogs bounded and jostled until they reached a patch of bushy ferns. Then Lucky paused, sniffing the air. He turned to Mickey. "The way we're headed, we'll have to pass quite close to the Fierce Dogs' lair."

Mickey's eyes widened. "Do we really have to? I managed to take another route and avoid it before."

"It's the fastest way back," Lucky whined. "I did this on the way to the city, and no dog challenged me. It'll be fine. But we must be quick and quiet, and very careful—just for a while."

Mickey shivered and his ears flattened. "So dogs are still living there?" He tilted his head in understanding. "It's a good thing we had our swim. The water probably helped to wash off our scents."

Lucky wasn't sure if that was true. Mickey seemed to smell even more strongly now that he was wet.

They padded on in silence, watchful for every cracking twig or crinkling leaf. Lucky remembered the last time he had passed near the lair. He tried not to think about the howls of pain as a dog had cried for mercy. It had sounded gravely injured—it was surely dead by now. *Mickey doesn't need to know about that. . . .*

As they curved around the Dog-Garden, Lucky was careful to keep their path upwind, hoping that this was enough to disguise their odors. But when they rounded the top edge of the Dog-Garden, Lucky heard a shrill yelp. He froze, his heart in his throat. Only a dog could have made that sound. He threw Mickey a warning look and they stood still as stones, ears pricked up.

There it was again! A high-pitched yap followed by plaintive whimpers. It was not the sound of a frightened dog but a vulnerable one.

"It's a pup," whispered Mickey. "More than one, maybe. . . ."

The Farm Dog was right. This wasn't the dog he'd heard howling in pain before. Lucky thought he could detect at least two small voices whimpering and whining in terror. He couldn't hear any grown dogs barking, or any sign that a Mother-Dog was close by.

Pity seized his chest. He longed to comfort the suffering pups. Where were their parents? Why would even the Fierce Dogs allow them to yowl like this without helping them? He shivered as he remembered the desperate yelps he had heard when he'd passed the Dog-Garden on the way to the city. The yelps that he had ignored. Tremors of guilt ran over his haunches. He had forgotten one of his Mother-Dog's lessons. He had let another dog suffer.

Oh, Forest-Dog. Please give me the instincts to know what to do. Almost as soon as he had finished his thought, the answer came to him. "They're in trouble. We have to help. . . ."

Mickey licked his chops nervously. "But the Fierce Dogs are so brutal. And how do we know that this isn't a trap? What if they are pretending to be pups to lure in smaller dogs?" He backed away a couple of paces, bumped into a tree trunk, and spun around, his eyes wild with fear. "We can't go into the Dog-Garden, Lucky. We *can't.*"

They listened to the whimpers a while longer. Lucky thought about what Mickey had said. He remembered the huge, brutish Fierce Dogs with their booming voices, their glossy coats, and ferocious jaws. He struggled to imagine that any of them could mimic these desperate, high-pitched squeals.

And even if they could, was that really something a Fierce Dog would do? Were they so cunning? Their Pack seemed much more fond of attacking directly rather than luring outsiders by trickery.

Lucky saw that Mickey was shaking with fear. How could he drag the black-and-white dog into danger? It would be so easy to sneak past the Dog-Garden. In no time he and Mickey would be lost in the expanses of the forest. If they hurried, they would be clear of the Wild Pack's old camp and far away by no-sun.

They would be *safe*.

Another high yap shattered Lucky's resolve. There were *pups* down there—frightened pups. They couldn't just leave them to die. . . .

But do I have the courage to save them?

CHAPTER NINE

The two dogs were silent, their ears pricked as they listened to the whimpers that rose from the Dog-Garden.

"They're pups," Lucky barked decisively. "We can't just ignore them."

Mickey crouched low to the ground, his tail limp behind him.

"But, Lucky," he whimpered, "they're *Fierce Dog* pups. Their nature is different from ours. They live to fight."

"Small ones can't hurt us," Lucky assured him with more conviction than he actually felt.

The Farm Dog shuddered. "Even if that's true, what about their Mother-Dog? She can't be far away. She's probably out hunting for them, and will be back soon. If she sees us near her pups . . ." His eyes flicked warily around him, drinking in the heavy foliage. It was hard to see beyond thickets and branches.

Lucky raised his snout. "I don't smell a Mother-Dog. I don't smell much. . . ."

"That's what worries me," said Mickey. "Doesn't it strike you as *strange*? There were so many dogs in their Pack, weren't there? And there are pups in their territory now. So others must be nearby. They'll be here before long."

Lucky wasn't so sure. Most of the scents of adult dogs were stale, with only a few fresher ones, and even they seemed a day old or more.

A high, desperate yip cut through the trees. Lucky's chest tightened and his whiskers shivered. He couldn't bear to hear that pitiful sound.

"What Mother-Dog could ignore that?" he asked Mickey. "Those pups are all alone."

"Fierce Dogs are different," Mickey whined. "Bella told me . . ."

Lucky's ears twitched. He thought about the Dog-Garden, with its short-cut grass and bowls of dried nuggets of meat. Bella, Daisy, and Alfie hadn't been able to believe their luck when they had found all that food—they hadn't realized that the area was guarded by a Pack of ferocious Fierce Dogs. Lucky winced when he remembered how he had watched, hidden, as the powerful black-and-brown dogs had strutted past on thickly muscled legs, their short, pointed ears pricked up and their lips curled into snarls. He remembered their sharp scents that radiated power and aggression.

He couldn't sense them now, though.

"We can at least see what's going on," said Lucky. "If it's dangerous, or we smell other dogs, I promise we'll get out of there right away. But we can't ignore pups in trouble. And who knows—they could be helpful."

"Helpful?" said Mickey doubtfully.

"In these strange times, every surviving dog has a role."

Mickey still looked unsure but he gave a quick, reluctant nod.

Creeping slowly over the soft forest floor, Lucky and Mickey approached the Fierce Dogs' territory, pausing regularly to sniff the air. The Sun-Dog was high overhead but his light was dim beneath the shade of the trees.

As they neared the fence, tension rippled along Lucky's back. Mickey was right—it *was* strange that there were no fresh scents from adult dogs. The tang of their sleek coats seemed old and faded, but it was still enough to make Lucky's heart thump in his chest and fear crackle beneath his fur.

The two dogs reached the high fence that enclosed the Dog-Garden. Lucky shuddered—such a sinister place, full of horrible memories.

They started circling it warily, seeking the gap where Daisy had dug a hole. Lucky let out a whimper when he found it—the hole was bigger now, much bigger. Stuck to the wire was a clump of glossy black fur.

"Fierce Dogs have been through here," Mickey whined.

Lucky knew they had. He had seen one near the fence when he'd heard those awful howls of pain. It was inevitable, really. The pointed-eared dogs must have grown used to coming and going as they pleased. Again Lucky caught the faded scent of the huge dogs, and a hint of something else—blood? He had to steady his hind legs, which were starting to tremble as he readied himself to walk back into the Dog-Garden.

He dipped and crawled beneath the wire, Mickey right behind him.

The Dog-Garden had changed since Lucky had last seen it. The neat, clipped lawn had vanished, replaced by high grass and creeping ivy. The shoots of trees had caught hold in a couple of places and thistles grew in spiky clumps. In time it would look like the rest of the forest, except for the low houses with their metal bowls. Lucky approached one. There were no hard nuggets of dry-looking meat in it. Perhaps the food had run out and that was why the Fierce Dogs had left.

"The longpaws haven't come back here," Lucky deduced. He had heard about Fierce Dogs before he had encountered them. The longpaws used them because they were ferocious, good at protecting their houses from intruders. Without longpaws to keep them caged and fed, the Fierce Dogs would have no one to control them, no one to tell them what to do. They would answer only to themselves. He tried to push this thought away, resisting the urge to turn on his paws and dash beneath the wire. The young dogs' whimpers were louder now. They seemed to be coming from the big house.

Lucky and Mickey skulked low in the long grass, treading toward the building, which was raised farther off the ground than the surrounding doghouses. Lucky climbed the wooden stairs to the front door while Mickey held back.

Lucky smelled the pups before he laid eyes on them. Their scent was like the one given off by Nose and Squirm—soft, sweet, and milky. The porch led all the way around the big house. Lucky crept along it, hugging the side of the building. He froze. Three Fierce Dog pups were wriggling in a chaotic bundle on a piece of soft-hide that reminded Lucky of the beds that the Leashed Dogs had been used to before the Big Growl. The pups were peering over the edge of the porch, blinking out at the wilderness. There were no low doghouses there, just grass growing long and wild. He could see the pups' little snouts and whiskers twitching. They knew that someone was near, though they hadn't spotted Lucky yet.

Memories of Lucky's encounter with the Fierce Dogs came back to him.

They could tell I was in their den, even though I stood upwind of them.

Did these pups share those sharp senses?

Like some of the grown Fierce Dogs, they had glossy tan-and-brown fur with darker faces and light muzzles, but these were rounder in shape and less threatening. Soft-furred, long ears hung at the sides of their heads, quite unlike the high, pointed ears of the adult Fierce Dogs.

Silently Lucky retraced his steps around the porch to where Mickey was waiting, out of earshot of the pups.

"There are three of them," he told Mickey. "They're all alone."

Mickey's eyes were huge. "There's something down there," he whined in a low voice.

Lucky tensed. "What do you mean?"

Mickey was trembling. Then Lucky caught it—a death scent, rising from the ground beneath their paws. He lowered his muzzle to the wooden floor. There was a narrow gap and through this Lucky could just see a dark, heavy bundle.

His nose twitched at the smell that rose up—a sour-sweet smell, like milk when it had been left in the sun.

Mickey whimpered: "I think it's their Mother-Dog."

Lucky gave an agreeing whine. "They're crying with hunger." His chest tightened with pity. For a moment he recalled his own Mother-Dog's sweet, silky fur, and the huddle of his littermates as they gathered around him. "And grief," he added softly, remembering the howls of pain he had heard when passing the Dog-Garden on his way to the city.

His ears drooped guiltily. Had the howls come from their Mother-Dog?

I did nothing to help her. . . .

Mickey nudged Lucky's face. "What if the other Fierce Dogs killed her?"

"Why would they do that?" Lucky asked, although he had already suspected the same thing.

Mickey looked out into the long grass. "I don't know. But then, why would they abandon the pups?"

Lucky had to agree—nothing the Fierce Dogs did made much sense. "I don't know, Mickey. But we have to go and talk to them, to make sure they're not in serious trouble."

Mickey nodded. "Okay, Lucky. You're right; we can't just leave them. But let's agree that if they're in trouble we will help them as quickly as we can, or take them with us if we have to. We don't want to hang around for the others to return."

"Of course," said Lucky. He stalked back along the edge of the porch with Mickey close behind him. As he turned the corner he saw the puppies huddled together. Their floppy ears pricked up, alert.

"I smell something!" yipped one of the pups, gnashing his small white teeth. The others whipped their heads around. Spotting Lucky and Mickey, they started barking in high-pitched voices

"Who are you? Go away!" yapped one.

"Our Pack will be back soon!" added another.

Mickey gave Lucky a worried look. "What if he's right?" he whined. "We don't want them to find us here."

"It's okay," Lucky told him. "The pup is bluffing. I don't think anyone else is here." Lucky studied the young dogs. He noticed that they had short, thin tails, unlike the adult Fierce Dogs, who only had stumps where their tails should be.

Mickey whimpered. "Maybe we're wrong to think we can help them."

Lucky was watching the pups, his head cocked. "Can't you see that they're frightened? We *have* to help them." He took a cautious step toward the pups, who gave off a series of fearful cries, snarls, and high-pitched squawks. Lucky spotted two bowls in front of their soft-hide. One had a puddle of water at its bottom; the other held a few crumbs of dried meat. Lucky dimly remembered that pups weren't supposed to go more than a few hours without food. They were probably starving.

He crouched in front of the pups, his posture low and unthreatening.

"My name is Lucky. My friend's name is Mickey. We want to help you. What are your names?"

The three pups stared at Lucky. Did they understand everything he'd just said? He had no idea.

"You're not part of our Pack! You shouldn't be here!" one of the male pups yapped.

"Don't you have names?" Lucky asked.

None of them answered.

Lucky watched them. If they didn't have names they had to be very young. They needed help—pups this young could not hunt for their food. They would starve to death very quickly.

He glanced at Mickey, who was standing a couple of paces behind him, then turned back to the pups. "We know you must be hungry," Lucky went on. "We will help you, but we can't stay here. There's nothing to eat. We'll take you somewhere safe, with lots of good food, and space to play in."

The female pup yipped, her eyes widening hopefully. Her thin tail gave a shy wag and she took a clumsy step toward Lucky. At her side, the smallest pup, a male, whined and licked his lips. He shook his head, revealing a tufty neck that gave him a softer appearance than his littermates.

Only the last pup, the stout male, still looked suspicious. "Go away! You're not supposed to be here!" he barked angrily. When Lucky approached he snarled and drew back. Lucky glanced beneath his paws at the wooden boards. Somewhere underneath this doghouse, the pups' Mother-Dog lay dead.

Their introduction to the world was the death of their Mother-Dog, thought Lucky, his chest tightening with sympathy as he remembered his own Mother-Dog. No wonder this pup was so distrustful.

"I understand," Lucky said, trying his best to sound calm despite a sudden urge to howl in pity. "Really, I do. I was separated from my Mother-Dog when I was a pup, just like you. I still miss her and think about her." He lowered his muzzle, his ears low.

Even the suspicious pup had stopped barking and all three of them watched Lucky with wide brown eyes.

"Your Mother-Dog has passed now," Lucky whined. "The best thing you can do is give her over to the Earth-Dog."

The pups watched him, confusion on their dark, pointed faces.

"Who is the Earth-Dog?" asked the female.

Mickey stepped forward to whine in Lucky's ear. "If their Pack's left them behind, we need to make sure they're with dogs who know how to look after pups. I think we should take them to the Wild Pack."

Lucky shuffled his paws apprehensively. If he wasn't welcome in the Pack by himself, how would Alpha react if he came back and brought three Fierce Dog pups with him? "They won't like it," he said slowly.

"No . . . but what else can we do?"

It's true, thought Lucky. *These pups need to be around dogs who understand how to take care of them. Dogs like Moon.*

Lucky touched Mickey's muzzle with his nose. "We'll bring them with us," he agreed.

He turned back to the pups. "The Earth-Dog is one of the

Spirit Dogs," he told them. "We can tell you about the Earth-Dog along the way."

"We have to stay here," the larger male growled.

"I don't want to leave Mother," added the female. "I don't want to give her to any dog!"

Lucky's chest tightened. He settled down in front of the pups. "I'm sorry. I know how hard this must be for you. I was so sad when I had to say good-bye to my Mother-Dog. But only Earth-Dog can look after her now."

The pups gazed at him, wide-eyed.

"Will we be able to see our Mother-Dog again if she's with the Earth-Dog?" asked the smallest male, who had hardly said a word until then. His short tail gave a hopeful wag and Lucky swallowed, grief crashing over him. How could he describe death to a pup? How could he explain things he barely understood himself?

"In a way," Mickey piped up. "You just need to close your eyes and remember. You won't *see* her . . . but you'll be able to *feel* her. She'll be all around you. In the earth beneath your paws, in the air you breathe. With the clouds in the sky and the sun and the rain."

Lucky's tail wagged at the memory of his own Mother-Dog, and the safety and warmth of the Pup-Pack.

"Can you show us how?" asked the female.

"Of course," said Mickey.

A lone crow cackled in the forest and the black-and-white dog flinched. "It's getting late," he murmured.

Lucky looked up to see a deeper blue beyond the wall of trees outside the Dog-Garden. The fur along his back prickled as he wondered, would the grown Fierce Dogs be back before no-sun? Would they be back at all? He turned to the pups. "We have a journey to go on, but for now, we need to get to work. Later Mickey will help you to remember your Mother-Dog. I promise."

The pups seemed to accept this. Lucky and Mickey led them to the wooden steps that took them from the porch to the ground. Mickey leaned forward to scoop up the largest male by the scruff but the pup squirmed free, shaking his tail and flanks proudly. He half jumped, half flopped down each step. His brother and sister followed, all three gathering in an excited cluster at the bottom.

The pups watched as Lucky found an earthy, shaded spot by the side of the big house where the grass was patchy. He started to dig as quickly as he could, pitching up dry soil. Mickey joined him.

After a few minutes of watching the digging in silence, the female pup drew closer. "What are you doing?" she asked.

Lucky stopped digging. "It's a ritual. We're going to offer your Mother-Dog to the Earth-Dog. It will help her to refind the earth and the air, to be part of the world again—but in another way, like Mickey said."

The female pup was silent. The smaller of her littermates stood shyly behind her, licking his chops and gazing at the shallow hole that Lucky and Mickey had dug in the ground. Only the larger male pup looked on with narrowed eyes.

Lucky was about to start digging again when he saw the female pup padding through the long grass and sniffing. He approached, his ears pricked up. He could now see that the pup was licking something that looked like a dark bundle next to a knot of ivy. It had been hidden in the grass.

Mickey followed his gaze and whined. He was standing nearer to the bundle and the female pup, and he watched her, fear crossing his eyes. "I think it's another pup. . . ." He addressed the female. "Come back, little one! Stay here."

The female pup looked up. "He's hurt. . . ." she whimpered.

"There's nothing you can do for him now," said Mickey.

Lucky winced. After a moment, the female pup abandoned the bundle and joined her brothers near the base of the big house.

Lucky trod through the grass to the small, limp body. Like the Mother-Dog, he had probably died a day or two before. The metallic scent of blood still clung to his fur. Lucky could make out the imprint of teeth—teeth shaped like his own—at the puppy's neck below an unusual blast of white fur that resembled the shape of a fang. Lucky gasped. The pup had been attacked and killed; that much was obvious.

If a coyote or a fox had killed him, they would have eaten him. But what sort of dog would do this to a pup?

Mickey's haunches were low as he pawed at the ground near the lifeless bundle.

"I don't like this, Lucky. What happened in this place?"

Lucky turned to his friend in acknowledgment. He couldn't imagine what had led to this pup and the Mother-Dog's death, and why the other Fierce Dogs had abandoned their camp, leaving the three other pups alone. But they could worry about that later.

"We have a duty to the dead dogs," Lucky whispered. "Even if they came from such a ferocious Pack, they deserve to be offered to the Earth-Dog."

The female pup called out to them. "Can you help him?"

The other two pups hung back. The small one kept his head low, his tail drooping; the larger one's eyes were narrowed, lips twitching as they curled over his vicious teeth, as though he was swallowing his own rage.

Lucky wished he could have shielded the pups from more sad

news. But he could do nothing. "I'm afraid I can't," he whimpered. "Was he your brother?"

"No!" yipped the larger male, his voice sharp. Lucky waited for him to say more but he just stood there on his sturdy little legs, glaring.

"Lucky, we should get out of here. . . ." Mickey whined.

The Farm Dog was right. Something strange—and awful— had happened in this Dog-Garden.

Crows swooped down to the high trees surrounding the camp. The Sun-Dog had started his slow descent along the horizon. Lucky returned to the shallow grave, digging until it was large enough for the Mother-Dog.

Mickey dug a much smaller hole alongside it for the dead pup. He took the limp body by the scruff and gently dragged him to the hole, laying him down carefully. Then he helped Lucky carry the Mother-Dog out from beneath the wooden boards. They gripped the heavy black collar at her neck and tugged with their teeth. She was incredibly heavy—Lucky could hardly believe that a dog could weigh that much. The hole they had dug was only just deep enough.

The three pups whined and yelped as Lucky and Mickey covered the dead pup's grave with soil, then attempted to do the same for the Mother-Dog. Lucky could hardly bear the sound of the pups' grief, and tried to swallow his sadness.

He and Mickey weren't able to move enough dirt to cover the Mother-Dog completely. Lucky stood for a moment, wondering what to do. Then he ran to the side of the camp to gather a mouthful of grass and leaves. He returned to the Mother-Dog, tossing his head to throw it over her body on top of the pile. He did this a couple of times until the dead Mother-Dog was reasonably well covered.

Lucky turned to the three pups. "The Earth-Dog will look after your mother now," he said solemnly.

"I don't *want* Earth-Dog to have her," whimpered the smallest male pup in a tiny voice.

The female leaned over and licked him on the ears. Lucky turned to peer into the long grass, wishing there was something he could do to ease their grief.

Mickey whined. Lucky turned back to him and spoke in a low voice so the pups couldn't hear. "What's wrong?" he asked.

"Everything's wrong," Mickey replied. His dark eyes scanned the sky. "The Sun-Dog is going to his lair. Are we really going to enter the forest with these three when it is *dark*?"

Lucky wished that he had another idea. But Mickey was right.

The forest at night is dangerous enough for a couple of adult dogs—how will we manage with three young pups to look after?

Lucky took a deep breath, and tried to keep the fear out of his bark. "The Forest-Dog will protect us. It isn't dark yet, and if we move quickly, we can cover a lot of ground before no-sun."

Forest-Dog! Please don't let these little pups come to any harm! he added silently. *They've already suffered so much.*

His eye caught the shape of the big house, eerie in the long shadows; then he turned to peer through the surrounding thickets and trees. They had a long journey ahead of them, and not much light.

The sooner they left this place of death, the better.

CHAPTER TEN

Twigs and leaves crunched under Lucky's paws as he led the others through the darkening forest. They had covered only the length of four rabbit-chases since leaving the Dog-Garden, and Lucky's flanks trembled as he thought about how much farther he and Mickey would have managed to walk if they were traveling alone. The pups were painfully slow, scrambling and struggling over each arching root or fallen branch. Their smaller legs tired out more quickly and they regularly stopped to fill their tiny chests with air. But they kept going bravely, encouraging one another with little yips.

"That's it," said the female, addressing her litter-brothers. "Great progress!"

"Think how far we've already gone," the larger male agreed.

Lucky was impressed by the pups' resilience. *I felt so bad about being forced out of the Pack. But if these pups can find the strength to keep going, after all they've been through, I can do the same. I can stop feeling sorry for myself.*

Their little tails shot up proudly but Lucky wasn't sure they would be able to walk much more. He spoke quietly to Mickey. "I think we should take turns carrying them, while the third pup walks between us."

Mickey looked warily at the stout, glossy-furred pups. "I think so too, but . . . they're Fierce Dogs. They seem proud. Do you think they'll let us?"

Lucky wasn't sure either. He turned to the pups. "You're doing really well," he told them. "But it's a bit uphill now. Would you let us take turns carrying you for a while?"

He watched the pups blink at one another. They stood stiff-legged and the female gave a hostile whine.

"Me and Lucky like to tease each other about who's the best at climbing uphill," Mickey said. "If we can each carry one of you it'll be good training for us."

"That's right!" Lucky blinked gratefully at Mickey, then looked at the pups. *Has he convinced them?*

Tentatively Lucky approached the larger, more suspicious male. The pup tensed but did not complain as Lucky sniffed his glossy coat, which hung in rolls around his neck, as if it belonged to a much larger dog. The pup stood still, trusting Lucky's delicate grip, as Mickey lifted up the other male and the plucky female walked between them. They struggled on through the forest, Lucky taking the lead with the heavier pup.

The pups don't seem to be as angry as the grown Fierce Dogs, thought Lucky. *Maybe that anger is something the longpaws have to teach them. That means these pups are no different from any other young dogs; they just need to be properly looked after.*

A little while later, Lucky heard the grumble of the smaller male's stomach. *I don't even know what these pups eat!* he realized. He remembered the crumbs of dried meat he had seen in the bowl on the porch. They could probably manage a mouse or a nice, juicy rat. His eyes scanned the forest, ears pricked for the sound of scurrying rodents as well as signs of danger.

Progress was difficult. Lucky and Mickey had to stop often and rest. Each time they resumed walking, they would swap pups, to make sure none of the little Fierce Dogs got too tired. Even so, their pace was slowing.

The large male was now walking between Lucky and Mickey. He paused at a broken branch on the forest floor, taking a deep breath before jumping over it. On the other side, he landed chaotically, losing his paws and rolling over to right himself. Lucky felt a twinge of pity—that must have taken more energy than the little dog was accustomed to using. He looked up between the branches to where the Sun-Dog was bounding a hasty retreat to his camp. Soon it would be no-sun.

"Let's stop for now," said Lucky, putting the female pup he had been carrying on the ground. Mickey gladly set down the smaller male and they all began to stretch and wash themselves.

Lucky approached the trunk of a gnarled old tree, sniffing and finding that the earth around it was dry and clean. They could curl up here in relative comfort.

"We aren't going to stay here, are we?" asked the larger male pup, gazing up at the sky. "What if it rains?"

Lucky turned his nose to the air. "I don't smell rain. We'll be fine. I don't want to keep walking in darkness unless we absolutely have to."

The pup scowled but didn't say any more. Lucky watched as he started to wash his short tail.

Lucky was about to say something about continuing their walk in the morning when he heard a rustling. Ears pricked up, he stalked toward a nearby hedge. Ignoring the sounds of Mickey and the pups as they stirred nearby, Lucky focused on the hedge.

He saw a glimpse of a velvety coat.

They would eat tonight after all!

Lucky and Mickey crouched down next to the pups, tearing the vole that Lucky had caught into small chunks. The pups watched, wide-eyed, their tails thrashing in excitement and anticipation. Lucky could taste the warm, tender meat and it was all he could do not to swallow the pieces down.

I had the last rabbit all to myself, he reminded himself sternly. *This is for the pups!*

First he lowered his head and offered a chunk of the vole to the smallest pup, who eagerly licked Lucky's muzzle and gobbled up the meat, crunching and gulping it down contentedly. Following Lucky's lead, Mickey offered some vole to the female, who took it from his jaws, her tail thrashing.

Lucky returned to the vole and took another careful bite, chewing it between his back teeth. The juice ran down his throat, and he could feel his belly opening to accept the delicious food—but, again, he resisted the urge to swallow it down. He approached the larger male, who bound toward him with his tongue lolling. The pup's suspiciousness seemed to have disappeared as he licked Lucky's muzzle, receiving the chunk of meat gratefully.

The pup turned to his smaller litter-brother. "It's your turn," he told him.

Lucky was touched by how supportive the pups were of one another, and how gently they received the food. As the smallest pup stepped forward, his short tail wagging, Lucky felt a twinge of pain in his chest.

These pups need us. . . . He peered at the surrounding trees. *Thank you, Forest-Dog, for delivering this meal, and for saving their lives.*

The little pup yelped happily, his body wiggling, rump moving this way and that as he licked Lucky's muzzle.

The pups finished the vole and curled up together contentedly, washing their paws. Mickey stood over them, stooping to lick their ears. He seemed much more at ease with them now. Lucky looked out into the forest. Even the crows had stopped cawing— it was almost no-sun, and the air thrummed with insects. He turned back to Mickey and the pups.

"There's something *very important* that we need to do," he announced solemnly. Mickey looked worried, until Lucky let his tongue loll playfully for just a moment. The Farm Dog relaxed, wagging his tail. Lucky went on: "We'll keep moving at sunup, but we really can't do that unless we find pup names for all of you."

The puppies looked at one another, then back to Lucky.

"When you're older, you'll get your real names, but you should have pup names for now. . . ." He turned to the smaller male, remembering how the little dog's rump had moved back and forth with happiness when Lucky had fed him a chunk of vole. "I think we'll call you 'Wiggle.'"

The pup responded by turning a tight circle, tottering on tiny legs. "Wiggle!" he echoed.

Lucky turned to the plucky female. "And you . . ."

Mickey piped up. "How about 'Lick'?"

"Yes, that's a good name," Lucky agreed.

The female's short black tail thrashed as she raised her muzzle to lick Mickey's nose. *I think she likes her new name,* Lucky thought happily.

He turned to the larger male. "As for you . . ."

The pup glared back challengingly, suspicious and guarded once more. "I don't need a 'pup name,'" he grunted.

Lucky thought for a moment. "We'll call you 'Grunt.' Yes, that's perfect."

Mickey barked his agreement and the other pups yelped happily, but the larger pup stayed still, his expression blank.

Lucky felt an odd sense of relief at having named the pups. He had come to care for them, even in this short time. It hadn't felt right when they were nameless. They were Lucky's responsibility now. He had rescued them because it had seemed like the right thing to do, to bring them back to the Wild Pack, but now . . .

Now I care.

With this contented thought, Lucky settled down near the three pups, back-to-back with Mickey.

Lick and Grunt slept soundly but Wiggle was shifting and fidgeting. Lucky leaned over and licked his ears.

The pup gazed up at him. "I can't sleep," he whimpered.

Lucky's heart twisted with pity. He thought of his days in the Pup-Pack. When he couldn't sleep, his Mother-Dog had drawn him close and he'd relaxed against the beat of her heart.

"Rest your head on my chest," Lucky murmured.

Wiggle shuffled close to him, burying his small dark head against Lucky. In moments he was breathing deeply, his eyes shut and his lips parted. Lucky closed his eyes too, but his ears stayed alert, listening to the sounds of the forest.

A howl echoed in the distance. Instantly Lucky sprang to his paws, eyes wide as he sniffed the cool night air. The pups yipped in alarm and Lucky was quick to silence them.

"It's okay," he soothed. "Whatever made that noise is far away.

But we need to be very quiet and not draw its attention."

"What *is* it?" Mickey asked. Lucky could just make out the Farm Dog's shape in the darkness.

"I'm not sure," Lucky told him. "It sounded like a dog, but not quite . . ."

Mickey gave a nervous whine. "A wolf?" he asked.

Lucky had heard wolves before, and he shuddered at the memory. "I hope not."

There was another long howl, which was joined by more voices. They seemed to be closer than the first howl. The hairs prickled along Lucky's neck and his heart thumped in his chest.

"There are lots of them!" whined Mickey.

"We'll be okay, but we must get moving." He nudged the pups with his snout and they scrambled to their paws, dazed and scared. "Mickey, you stay to one side of the pups, and I'll be on the other." He sniffed the air but could not pick up a scent.

"Have they smelled us?" asked Lick.

"No, I don't think so," Lucky murmured. "They don't know we're here."

"You're not going to leave us, are you, Lucky?" Wiggle whimpered.

"We're going to be by your sides the whole time," Lucky

promised. "There's nothing to fear. Just stay quiet and keep moving—we'll soon find somewhere safe to rest." Lucky hoped he sounded reassuring, even though he was telling them a lie. The creatures they had heard sounded large and dangerous.

No dog spoke after that. They walked silently through the forest, the pups scrambling over fallen leaves, twigs, and thorns. Lucky knew it was hard for them, but he wanted to keep all his senses sharp and it would be easier to do that if he was not carrying a pup.

He could smell a sharp odor in the air—it smelled a little like wolf-stink, and also fox, but something told him these creatures were neither.

And a cold fear told him that whatever they were, they had caught the dogs' scent. He could hear leaves crunching beneath paws, could smell the sharp odor getting closer.

"Wait!" Mickey yelped, as he stalked low behind the pups.

Lucky turned to him quickly. "What's wrong?"

"It's Wiggle. He's falling behind."

"He's really tired," yipped Lick. "He's not used to walking this fast, or this far." Lucky guessed that none of the pups were, but the female's eyes flashed with proud resilience, and Grunt jutted his pointy snout out alongside her.

Lucky was ashamed that he had not noticed. Now he could hear the smallest pup's labored panting. Mickey and Lick were right—Wiggle was tired.

"Here," he said gently. "I'll carry you for a while. Mickey, you will need to be my eyes and ears." The black-and-white dog dipped his head in acknowledgment, a shadow of dark fur against branches. Then Lucky scooped up Wiggle gently between his jaws. They all froze as they heard a strange voice.

"This way!" The voice was nasal and brassy. Lucky felt his whole body turn to stone.

"Smells dogsie-pets, smells them close."

"Cubs! Smells cubs!"

Lucky's heart lurched and he almost dropped Wiggle in shock. He knew what they were now—a Pack of these beasts had once entered the city, snarling and growling. Only longpaws carrying sticks had been enough to chase them away.

Coyotes! Those fierce, sneaky creatures that feast on frail animals. They're swift and spiteful too. They must have picked up the smell of pups. They think they're onto an easy meal.

"Stay quiet," he told the others. Then he lifted his snout into the air as he tried to untangle the coyotes' scents. *Six of them, at least.* More than enough to isolate and overwhelm Lucky and

Mickey—and more than enough to steal a pup.

I cannot let these pups end up like Fuzz, Lucky thought with a pang of anguish.

"We need to pick up the pace," he urged.

"I smell them too," Mickey whispered. "Do you think we can outrun—"

Lucky gave a quick shake of his head to silence the Farm Dog. He didn't want to say the word *coyote* in front of the pups; it would only scare them. Mickey blinked once, to show his understanding. Lick and Grunt pranced forward, scrambling over the jumble of debris on the forest floor. They passed through a tunnel of narrow-trunked trees at the top of a low hill before dipping toward denser foliage.

If we can get downwind of them in the deep forest we may be able to lose them.

They made good progress, and Lucky thought his plan was going to work. But then he heard Lick panting and whimpering behind him. He looked back and saw that she was struggling over the rough ground. Her latest surge of energy seemed to have run dry. Even Grunt was showing signs of weariness, his short tail hanging low as he trudged on determinedly.

"This won't work," Mickey murmured. He was even lower to

the ground now, his body melting into the sinews of the forest. "I think they're after the pups. We should all mask our scents, then hide and wait for them to pass."

Lucky nodded. "How do we—"

"Hide?" Grunt snarled. "A Fierce Dog *never* hides!"

Lucky's ear twitched. So Grunt knew they were different from other dogs. What else did the pup know?

Mickey ignored him, diving down into the dirt and mulch of the forest floor, where he rolled repeatedly. Then he sprang to his paws and pressed against the trunk of a nearby tree, rubbing his back, tail, and muzzle.

Lucky was impressed. He hadn't expected Mickey to have such clever survival skills. The Farm Dog had come a long way since they had first met in the city.

He imitated Mickey, dropping low and rubbing his belly against fallen leaves. "Pups, do what we do. And you must resist the urge to wash yourselves."

The puppies started rolling, kicking up dirt. Even Grunt cowered down and buried his snout beneath some leaves, allowing Lucky to cover him with twigs and soil.

"That's good," whispered Mickey. "Now we need to be very quiet and very still." He took the lead, scrambling beneath a bush, flattening himself on the forest floor. "Come close," he added. Lick did as she was told, squeezing her body next to Mickey's, little Wiggle at her side.

Grunt made no move to lie down. "I'm not hiding from any dog," he snarled. He started to walk away from the bush, toward the low hill with its gateway of thin-trunked trees.

"Where's go cubs?"

"Close, cohorts. Smell cubs . . ."

Lucky choked back a whimper of fear, lunging toward Grunt and shoving him into the undergrowth. The pup struggled and Lucky threw his weight against him, feeling Grunt's muscles rippling and flexing beneath his fur. He was already a very strong dog.

"Your bravery is admirable, Grunt," Lucky murmured, his muzzle at the pup's ear. "But this isn't the time. These aren't dogs; they're coyotes looking for a fight. We have to stay silent. This is serious."

Lucky felt the pup shudder. "Coyotes? What are they?" he asked, as the beasts drew nearer, rounding the low hill.

"I eats the cubs. Starts with the tender snouts!" hissed one of the coyotes in its raspy voice.

"I crunch the tails!" added another.

Grunt started trembling. Lucky felt a wave of compassion for him—the tiny Fierce Dog acted tough, but he was just a pup, feeling a pup's fear.

Please, wise Forest-Dog, thought Lucky. *These pups have already lost their Mother-Dog. Let them get through this night. . . .*

The coyotes gathered at the top of the hill among the tall trees, sniffing and circling. They had thickly furred bodies like wolves, and their legs were long and narrow. Their large pointed ears cut jagged outlines on the dark horizon and their sharp smell turned Lucky's stomach. He remembered Old Hunter telling him about coyotes as they rested by the Food House in the city—how they were sneaky, opportunistic killers, known to eat sharpclaws and snatch pups from their Mother-Dogs. Well, they weren't getting *these* pups!

"They're heres . . . Smells young dogs."

"Not heres . . . Escapes. Escapes, Mangles, how?"

"This ways; they gone. Cohorts, follow!"

The last coyote that spoke—the one called Mangles—was particularly tall. Its shape was lithe and wiry as it spun on its paws. Its tail was a stump of fur, as though it'd lost the end of it somehow. It started running back through the thin-trunked trees, down the hill toward the path.

If they hold the scent, Lucky thought hopefully, *they will eventually be taken all the way to the Dog-Garden....*

Soon the coyote Pack had disappeared from sight and finally even their sharp, peaty odors had faded on the night air.

When he was certain that the danger had passed, Lucky rose to his paws.

"They've gone," he said, panting with relief.

"What *were* they?" asked Mickey. "They looked like Alpha, but thinner."

"Coyotes," replied Lucky with a shudder. "I don't know much about them."

"I already know more about them than I want to," Mickey barked. He gazed out through the dark tangles of vines and branches. "We should keep moving."

Lucky turned to the pups. "You all did really well, and I'm sorry that we won't be able to go back to sleep just yet. We need to keep moving until the Sun-Dog appears. We'll take it slowly, and we'll look out for one another. The Pack of dogs that we're going to meet has a camp by a large lake, under some rocks. There'll be shelter and food there. What do you say?"

Grunt was the first on his paws, nudging his sister and brother. "Come on, you two!" he yipped as they rose more slowly.

Lucky led the way, with Mickey dropping to the back of the group, watching in case the coyotes reappeared.

Lucky focused on sniffing out a safe route through the trees. When he turned back to check on the pups he was pleased to see how helpful Grunt had become, encouraging his littermates with shunts of his snout and enthusiastic licks.

Lucky was grateful, but he still felt ill at ease. They'd survived their encounter with the coyotes, but Grunt had refused to hide. Lucky remembered how the pup had squirmed beneath him. *He doesn't like taking directions,* Lucky thought. *And he has more energy than he knows what to do with.* Grunt was a survivor—Lucky could see that—but he was also a risk taker.

And taking risks could get a dog killed.

CHAPTER ELEVEN

Lucky sank onto his belly on the rough soil at the bottom of the rocky overhang. It was where the united Pack had settled after their journey through the forest. He'd worked so hard to get the pups here, and now . . .

It was deserted.

He scanned the area, searching for signs of the Pack, and let out a long whine, his tail limp and his ears low. The Pack had disappeared. There was no dog to greet him, no yaps or barks. Even Alpha, with his snarling, wolfish face, would have been something.

Mickey appeared at Lucky's side, sniffing the rocky earth.

"Where have they gone?" asked the black-and-white dog. Lick, Grunt, and Wiggle stood behind him, panting.

Lucky sighed. "I don't know . . . they must have left not long after I did. There's barely any trace of them."

Lick sprang up to Lucky excitedly. "Is there food here?" she yapped, glancing around.

Lucky didn't answer and Mickey brushed past him, stepping beneath the overhang, trailing his muzzle over the ground, stopping to sniff deeply or lick the occasional clump of dirt or pebbles. Lucky watched him, noticing the scuffle of paw marks in the dirt. He tried to match them to different Pack members. There were large, heavy imprints that he thought could have been Martha's, but the rest were unclear. A smudge of small prints cut through some other marks, then vanished in a muddle of soil: Sunshine? Daisy? It was pointless trying to guess.

Lucky could scarcely bear to lift his head. He had made a point of waking the others before the Sun-Dog reached its highest point, leading them back to the Pack's camp. As Wiggle had whimpered about his sore paws, Lucky had raised the pup's spirits by telling him tales of Packmates to play with, and more food than he could eat. It hadn't exactly been the truth—the Pack had complained about the grainy soil and absence of prey—but he had hoped they would have settled in and found some by now.

"You'll love the Pack," Lucky had told the pups. "Martha will teach you how to swim and Fiery is a great hunter. You'll learn a lot from him." It had twisted his gut to talk of the Pack, but what choice did he have? He had to make sure that the pups took to their new home. Without the safety of other dogs, they would be dead in days; he was sure. That was assuming that the Pack even agreed to take the young dogs. Lucky hadn't allowed himself to consider the possibility that they would not. But surely, even if the Pack didn't want Lucky back, they would never refuse these motherless pups.

How could the Pack just have vanished? Lucky thought with a shiver. The abandoned shelter looked dark and empty beneath the overhang without the flurry of other dogs. Wiggle scampered closer, wide-eyed.

"You said it was safe," he yipped, his short tail hanging between his legs. "It doesn't *look* very safe to me."

"I know; I'm sorry," Lucky replied. "When we left the whole Pack was here. We should be able to pick up their scents; we can follow them."

But in his head, he added: *Do these pups have the strength to keep going? And could there be danger nearby? Is that why the Pack seems to have left in such a hurry?*

Lucky swallowed a whimper and rose abruptly to his paws, shaking off the sense of dread that coursed through his tired limbs. He approached Wiggle, licking the top of the pup's head.

"The camp has been moved," he told him, "but we'll find it—won't we, Mickey?"

The Farm Dog barked in agreement. "I think I've picked up their scent-trail. They seemed to have walked along the edge of the lake. They left together, as a whole Pack. That's good news, isn't it? The Leashed Dogs and the Wild Pack must have set aside their differences after all."

Wiggle dipped his head in resignation and went to join Lick and Grunt, who had found a flat stone by the lake and were stretching out in the sun.

Lucky watched the puppy walk away. He didn't answer the Farm Dog's question, thinking of the confrontation between Bella and Sweet the morning that he'd been expelled.

"Come on, Lucky. If we hurry, we can catch them by no-sun." Mickey butted Lucky's head cheerfully, then paused. "What's wrong?"

Lucky's head drooped. "They may not want me to follow them."

"What do you mean?"

"I left the Pack, Mickey."

The black-and-white dog gazed at him without understanding. "So we were wrong. We'll say sorry; we'll explain." He cocked his head. "We've been over this. Why do you look so worried?" He glanced at the pups. "You can't abandon us, Lucky. Not now."

Lucky met his friend's eye though his tail hung low. "You *chose* to leave. It was different for me. I was driven out by Alpha." He lowered his voice so the waiting pups couldn't hear. "He said I was a traitor and that the Pack would be better off without me."

Mickey frowned. "What nonsense. Of course it isn't! You're the bravest, cleverest dog I know." He licked Lucky's muzzle. "Alpha's just intimidated by you, scared of any challenge to his leadership. He's not half the dog you are! Some dogs would have left the pups in the Dog-Garden, but you didn't. Being with you gives me courage. You'll just have to reason with Alpha. You'll manage it, too—you could charm the rabbits out of their burrows!"

"I'll try my best," Lucky murmured, touched but not convinced.

A few dog-lengths away, the bored pups had started playfighting. Grunt pounced on Wiggle and they rolled in the dirt, growling. Lick snapped her chops around the stems of some wild flowers, chewing, then spitting them out, her face scrunched up.

"Urgh! They're horrible!"

Wiggle scrambled free of Grunt. "When will we have real

food?" he whined, smacking his lips. "I'm hungry!"

"Me too," Grunt echoed.

"We'll find some food soon," said Lucky vaguely.

"How about them?" yapped Grunt, bounding toward the lake. He stood at the bank, barking at the waterbirds. Out on the water, the birds turned wary heads toward the pup but soon resumed their indifferent *clacks*.

Lucky eyed the birds, but he knew it would be impossible to catch them. "We'll get another vole, or maybe even a rabbit. We just need to be patient and see what the Forest-Dog offers us." Not that he'd seen any rabbits all day—but there had to be *something* here. He started sniffing his way around the edge of the camp. Mickey was right: The other dogs had followed the bank of the lake, away from the forest and the Fierce Dogs' lair with its ominous smells of death and emptiness. Lucky cast a last look in that direction. Far beyond the forest lay the city that had once been his home. With a jolt he remembered the giant loudbirds and wondered if they'd flown this way—perhaps that was why the Pack had left?

"Who's the Forest-Dog?" asked Lick. She skipped along the edge of the overhang, chasing ants.

Lucky blinked at her in surprise. "Sometime I'm going to have to sit you pups down and tell you all about the Spirit Dogs."

"Does the Forest-Dog make food for us?" asked Wiggle in his small, high voice.

"He doesn't *make* food, but he watches over the trees and animals. He protects us, you see. He keeps dogs safe, and if he is pleased he offers us delicious morsels like vole and rabbit. So it's important to remember the Forest-Dog, and to be grateful to him. If you're hungry, you might say: 'Please deliver me some food, wise Forest-Dog.' And once you've caught and eaten a vole, you would say 'Thank you, Forest-Dog.'"

Wiggle exchanged a puzzled look with Grunt, who was padding toward them. Lick paused, her dark brow wrinkled in thought. "But if the Forest-Dog watches over the trees and animals, doesn't that mean he watches over voles and rabbits too?"

"Where does the Forest-Dog sleep?" asked Wiggle, shaking his floppy ears. "Does he have a camp? It must be really, really big. He must be a giant to see so much."

"We're not even *in* the forest," Grunt pointed out. "Most of the trees have gone. Doesn't it take more than one or two trees to make a forest?"

The memory of a stormy night came back to Lucky. He, too, had asked his Mother-Dog questions about the Spirit Dogs, desperate to understand the great and mysterious world around him, and she had answered, telling him all about the Sky-Dogs and Lightning.

"That's true," Wiggle put in. "Forests have *lots* of trees." The smallest pup panted happily, as though he had made an incredible discovery.

Lucky's tail started wagging—the pups had a point. He glanced at the lone tree with a mottled silver bark that stood some distance away around the rocky overhang. He'd forgotten what it was like to look at the world with such curiosity and inno-cence. Now memories flooded back to him, of a time when he was called Yap, play-fighting with his litter-sister Squeak. She used to ambush him, sneaking up from behind and chewing playfully on his ear.

With a surge of happiness, Lucky spun around and nipped Wiggle gently on his tufty neck. Grunt yapped cheerfully and started running along the bank, back toward the overhang.

"You won't catch me!" he cried. The pup's short legs thundered against the sandy ground and for a moment he had a clear lead before Lucky gained on him. With a friendly growl, he pounced on Grunt and the pup yipped and snarled as Lucky licked his face. He felt Wiggle nip at his legs as he came up behind. All of them ended up rolling and play-fighting.

Lucky panted happily. It was wonderful to see the pups so mischievous and full of energy.

He was hardly aware of Lick until he heard Mickey's voice, warning her: "You'll never reach it!"

Lucky looked up to see Lick quite far away, around the other side of the overhang, running at full pelt. A flash of gray fur shot in front of her.

"I've almost got it!" yapped Lick excitedly.

Lucky saw it was a squirrel she was chasing, and that the little animal was making for the silvery tree. She hurtled after it, her paws a blur as she kicked up soil.

She's going too fast; she'll slam into the trunk!

"Stop her!" barked Lucky in alarm, starting after Lick. His heart leaped to his throat and his paws pounded beneath him.

Mickey was closer to the tree and he made a dash for it, but the squirrel got there first. It burrowed into a hole at the base of the tree, disappearing from sight. Lick bounded after it, diving toward the hole just as Mickey reached the tree. At first it looked as though Lick would squeeze inside the hollow after the squirrel, her head and forepaws disappearing through the gap, but she stopped abruptly.

Half of Lick's body was inside the tree. Her back legs hung out of the gap, kicking desperately, her body twisting and jerking.

"She's trapped!" Mickey whined.

Lucky skidded to a halt by the tree and brought his head close to the base of the trunk. "Lick? Lick, can you hear me? Try not to struggle; we'll have you out in no time."

The pup bucked at the sound of his voice, her tail spinning. Lucky felt sick at the fear scent rising from her small body.

"It's okay; we're here," he assured her. He turned to Mickey. "Keep her still!"

Mickey lay his long snout and neck across Lick's back and gently pressed her down. Her tail still twitched and jerked, but her body and back legs were held in check as Lucky started scrabbling at the bark of the trunk, trying to force it to widen. It was much harder than he had imagined. It was nothing like digging against soil—the bark was tough and solid.

Grunt and Wiggle stood a short distance away, yipping desperately.

"Our litter-sister!" Wiggle cried.

"Lick!" barked Grunt. "Lick! You have to get out of there!"

The little dog trapped inside the tree trunk must have heard as she shunted against Mickey, her tail jerking wildly.

"Stay calm!" urged Mickey, addressing all the pups at once, though Grunt and Wiggle continued to scamper about frantically.

Lucky ignored them, scratching away at the trunk until a splinter of wood came free. It wasn't enough. . . .

"She's not struggling as much!" barked Mickey, his voice trembling with fear. Lucky pulled back. Lick's tail had fallen limp.

She can't breathe!

Lucky abandoned his efforts at the wooden trunk, sliding his paw beneath Lick's body and jabbing at the soil at the base of the gap. This started to come away and he dug and scraped feverishly. He knew he had to be quick—even now Lick's hind legs were slumping on the ground behind her. He clawed the ground until his paws throbbed with exhaustion and pain shuddered through his limbs. Then all of a sudden Lick toppled back out of the hole and fell gasping on the ground.

Lucky and Mickey yelped in relief, washing her small tan face. Grunt and Wiggle joined in, shunting their litter-sister affectionately.

Grunt turned to Lucky and licked his muzzle. "You saved her! Thank you!" he yipped, before turning back to Lick. Wiggle didn't say anything but he nuzzled his head against Lick's side protectively.

Lucky flopped onto the grainy earth beside them, panting as the tension quivered out of each hair and whisker. He felt a hot surge in his chest as he realized that he would do whatever he needed to in order to keep them safe.

Mickey dropped down next to him with a whine. "That was close!"

"Too close," Lucky sighed. He was finally beginning to relax. He watched the pups from the corner of his eye. They were now walking about in a tight, writhing circle, nipping and licking one another as though nothing had happened. *They're so lighthearted and full of energy. Was I like that once?*

The sound of paws crunching over earth caught Lucky's ears and he leaped up, ears cocked. Something was creeping through the long grass by the bank of the lake. The rhythm of the pawsteps was unmistakable: It was a dog! Lucky puffed himself up to his full height. His eyes shot to the pups, who were still playing a couple of long-strides away. He made a silent oath that he wouldn't let anything happen to them. Even if the Pack wouldn't let him back in, he'd escort the pups as far as he could. If danger was coming, this time he would be ready.

CHAPTER TWELVE

The long grass parted and a small, fluffy, white head appeared.

Daisy!

She barked excitedly, spinning, bounding across the grass, and leaping in the air.

"Lucky! Lucky! I knew you'd come back! And you brought Mickey, too!"

Lucky felt a burst of happiness. He bounded toward her with Mickey at his side. "Daisy!" he barked, his tail thrashing the air. "We thought you'd all left!"

She lowered her head as Lucky and Mickey leaped around her, giving her delighted licks. "I'm so sorry," she whined. "We should never have let you go. . . ."

"We came back, but you'd disappeared!" Mickey told her.

Daisy raised her head, her eyes sparkling. "They said you were gone for good, but I knew you would come back!" she barked. "I just knew—" Her happy howl died away as her eyes settled on something behind Lucky and Mickey.

Lucky spun around. The three pups were watching.

Daisy whined and took a step back. "What are *they* doing here?"

Wiggle trotted up to stand beside Lucky, but did not take his eyes off Daisy. Lucky greeted him with a lick to the nose.

"I can smell fear. . . ." Wiggle whined. "Just like Mickey when he first met us."

Mickey heard him and took a step toward the pup. "I'm not scared anymore," he soothed.

"But you were at first," Wiggle barked. "Why were you scared of us?"

Mickey looked to Lucky, who was thinking about what to say. *How do we tell them that their parents were killers?* Grunt seemed to know that he was a Fierce Dog—but did he understand *everything* that meant?

The larger male pup trod past them toward Daisy, who backed away. Her fear scent wafted on the air.

Grunt growled: "It's because we're getting bigger every day. Soon we will be huge, just like Mother and the other dogs in our camp. Then no dog will dare to challenge us." Although his voice was thin and high, Daisy shrank, her tail clinging to her flank.

Lucky felt a shiver run through his body. *So he does understand,* he thought.

"Lucky," Daisy whined, staring hard at him, "did you *steal* Fierce Dog pups?"

"It wasn't like that. We brought them with us because we had no choice," he answered.

"You took them from the Dog-Garden? After what happened when we were trapped there? Don't you remember how *vicious* those dogs were?"

Lucky took a step toward Wiggle, who looked bewildered. He nudged the pup with his nose and looked back at Daisy. "There were no adult dogs in the garden, Daisy. Only the pups. We couldn't just leave them there."

"Why not? Surely the Fierce Dogs wouldn't have left their pups alone for long. They'll start searching! Won't they be furious? They'll want revenge against the dogs who stole their pups!" She shuddered, her ears twitching with nerves.

"We're right here, you know," Lick murmured. "We can hear you!"

"Honestly, Daisy, it's fine," Lucky assured her, stepping along-side Grunt. "The Dog-Garden was empty. The Fierce Dogs' scent was stale—they were not coming back. These little pups were starving and their Mother-Dog was"—he caught himself just in time—"with the Earth-Dog."

Daisy nodded in understanding, though she still looked uncertainly at Grunt.

Lucky went on. "We couldn't leave them there to starve. Any dog would have done the same." He dipped his head to nuzzle Grunt between the ears. The pup didn't respond, his body stiff as he glared at Daisy.

I hope he doesn't do anything impulsive, Lucky thought, remembering how the pup had wanted to confront the coyotes.

Daisy took a tentative step toward them, but froze when Grunt's lip curled back and a thin snarl escaped his throat.

"It's okay," murmured Lucky, lowering his snout to Grunt's ear. "Daisy is a friend; she's from the Pack."

"She doesn't *seem* like a friend," Lick whined.

"A friend doesn't say such mean things," added Wiggle dejectedly.

Grunt fell silent, though his lips were still parted.

"Where did every dog go?" Mickey asked, casting an eye back at the rock overhang and the peaceful lake. "Why aren't you with the others?"

"After you left, Alpha sent Beta, Fiery, and Snap out to explore. I think he was worried about food, because we hadn't scented any prey near the camp. Spring thinks that the ground around here is too rocky for rabbits to dig their tunnels, which is why we don't see them. So we moved to a new territory beyond the lake, by a river. It could be the same river that passes through the forest; I'm not sure. It smells clean and sweet, and the water is delicious."

Lucky gave a nod, relieved that the Pack's decision to move had nothing to do with the giant birds. He wondered at how casually Daisy spoke about members of the Wild Pack—like they were old companions. *It hasn't taken her long to adapt to Alpha's rules,* he thought with a twinge of resentment, wondering what he would find when they were finally reunited with the Pack. Had they shared the Great Howl in his absence, weaving Leashed and Wild Dog closer together?

Daisy scratched her ear with a hindpaw. "They all said you were both gone for good, but I knew you would return! I've come here a couple of times to check. I couldn't smell anything until now." Her happy barks became sad: "Oh, Lucky, I really am so sorry that you left. The Pack is going to be so happy to see you both! Bella, Martha, everyone!"

Lucky looked to the lake. *They won't all be happy that I'm back.* His mind strayed to Sweet, and he tried to imagine how she would respond. His chest tightened with sadness as he remembered that angry glimmer in her eyes. Would she ever forgive him?

"Lead the way," he told Daisy, forcing lightness into his yelp.

The little dog turned on her short legs and began retracing her steps through the long grass, looping around the water. Lucky stood aside so that the pups could go ahead of him with Mickey. Wiggle scampered past, his wagging tail a perfect target for Lick, who nipped at her litter-brother.

Grunt walked just ahead of Lucky, his tail straight behind him, ignoring his littermates. He glanced back once, his expression blank—*empty.*

A crackle of nerves ran through Lucky's bones. He wondered how Grunt would handle life in a large, mixed Pack. *He doesn't like being told what to do . . . and he certainly doesn't enjoy being questioned.* If the pup challenged Alpha the way he had stood up to Daisy, there could be serious consequences.

But for who?

CHAPTER THIRTEEN

A row of pines masked the air with their sweet fragrance, but Lucky could already pick out the scents of Pack members as they drew nearer to the riverbank. His tail gave a wag as he realized that Martha was close. It drooped when his nose detected the musky odor of a half wolf. . . .

Alpha.

Daisy pawed the ground, then turned an excited circle. "It's beyond those trees. You'll love it! The shelter is really safe and warm; it's a large cave and there are sharp vines hanging over the entrance to scare off intruders. Oh, Lucky—everyone is going to be so happy to see you!"

Lucky wasn't so sure about that. But they hadn't come this far to turn back now. He lowered his head to address the pups:

"You three rest here for a while. I'll come back for you soon. I just need to explain to the others that you're here."

Wiggle stared at him. "You aren't going to leave us, are you, Lucky?"

"They won't want us," said Lick.

"They'll be *scared*," added Grunt, casting an accusing eye after Daisy as she bounded off through the trees.

"They won't be scared, and they *will* want you," Lucky assured them all. "Just wait here, and I'll come and get you." He gave them each a quick lick of the head before turning to follow Daisy and Mickey through the trees.

I hope I'm right, he thought.

"So the wanderers return."

Alpha's yellow gaze was icy, sending prickles of anxiety along Lucky's back.

Lucky turned away slightly as he looked at the circle of dogs. Bella hung her head as she stood beside Dart and Spring. Large, patient Martha's tongue lolled between her great jowls. Sweet was very still, her long face blank and her soft ears low. Bruno stood next to her, his tail hanging between his legs.

"What's going on?" Nose yipped, but Moon silenced him with a nuzzle of her snout. Her ears fell and she exchanged a look with Fiery.

They feel bad about how they treated me, Lucky realized. *Well, let them! They allowed Alpha to drive me away. It's right that they feel shame.*

The only dogs who looked *pleased* to see him were Snap, her wiry tail lashing the air, and little Whine, whose eyes glinted happily.

Lucky had only been away for a few journeys of the Sun-Dog, but it seemed like much longer. He felt every bit an outsider as he realized that the Leashed and Wild Dogs stood in a mixed group. When had they become so comfortable with one another?

He turned to look at Mickey, who was standing low to the ground, waiting for someone to speak. The Farm Dog's coat was shiny against the soft grass beneath his paws. The meadow was bursting with life. Birds twittered overhead and Lucky could smell warm rabbit droppings. Here, Lucky knew he would be able to keep the promises he had made to the Fierce Dog pups about how well they would eat.

He was impressed by the new camp. The Pack had found a good spot at the foot of a sloping hill, guarded from the wind by surrounding pines and with access to clean river-water. A small meadow rolled down to some distant rocks, the rich smell of wild flowers rising on the breeze. Beyond the rocks, the forest began once more, a blur of green leaves. It was a fragrant, peaceful place.

And they had settled here without him. A pang of sorrow tightened in Lucky's throat but vanished when he returned Alpha's gaze.

The half wolf sneered at him, his lip peeling back to reveal his teeth. "Couldn't you and your house-pet survive on your own?"

Behind him, Lucky heard Mickey give a soft whine.

"Where's your longpaw toy, *house-pet?*" mocked Alpha.

Mickey stiffened. "I left it behind." He licked his chops. "I was mistaken in thinking that the longpaws had returned—the city is just as bad as we left it . . . worse."

Daisy and Martha nodded sadly.

"I was wrong to leave," the black-and-white dog went on. "I would like to"—he glanced at Lucky—"that is, *we* would like to join the Pack again."

Alpha's muzzle wrinkled, revealing a glint of ivory fang. "If you need the Pack so much, you had better be prepared to *prove* it." He jutted his long snout forward.

He means we should be prepared to grovel, thought Lucky, feeling his hackles rising. *Well, I won't grovel before a coward who fell apart at the sight of a black cloud!* He took a deep breath, trying to shake away his frustration, remembering the three pups who were waiting alone outside the camp: It was not the time to start arguments.

Alpha took a step closer. His eyes were fixed on Lucky. His top lip trembled and spit hung off it, gliding down his shiny fangs. "Prove it, city rat! *Prove* that you need us!"

Lucky was not going to cower before the half wolf. He raised himself up to his full height and opened his mouth to growl back a reply. But before he could, they were interrupted by a volley of high-pitched yaps.

Lucky spun around. Sunshine had shimmied her way through the circle of dogs to appear between Lucky and Alpha.

"Fierce Dogs!" she yapped breathlessly. "I can smell them, can't you? Fierce Dogs are close!"

A wave of nervous barks and yelps coursed through the Pack. Fiery pressed closer to Nose and Squirm, growling. Sweet sniffed the air as little Whine whimpered, his curly tail trembling.

"I smell them, too," snarled Sweet.

Alpha sprang forward, his gray fur puffed up so that he looked almost twice his size. "Where are they? Where are the monstrous cowards? Show yourselves!"

As he turned to face the pine trees, Lucky caught Mickey's anxious gaze. Their return to the camp was not going the way they had hoped.

"There's nothing to worry about," Lucky barked above the

noise of the Pack. "It's three little pups. We brought them with us."

Alpha shot around. "You *brought them?*"

"Lick! Grunt! Wiggle! Come here," Lucky called.

The Pack watched as the pups emerged from between the trees. Led by Lick, they walked through the long grass toward Lucky.

Bella, Dart, and Spring fell back to let the pups pass. Bruno scrambled behind Daisy, while Whine hid his head in his paws.

Lucky's heart sank. He supposed he should have known after Mickey's and Daisy's reaction to the pups, but he'd hoped for more from his old Packmates. *These dogs lived through the Big Growl— and they're scared of three tiny pups?*

Snap dropped to her haunches, her ears pressed back and her lips quivering. She was usually so easygoing. Lucky stepped around the pups, standing side-on to the hunting dog—he did not like the look on her face. Grunt sniffed in Snap's direction and scowled. Lucky wondered if he had sensed the hostility rising from her fur.

"What were you thinking, foolish City Dog?" Alpha rasped. "Is this how you take your revenge on me—by bringing evil, vicious creatures to our camp?"

Lick whimpered and Lucky could not contain his snarl. "They're just pups! Their Mother-Dog is dead, and their Pack left them in their lair to die."

"Where is their lair?" whined Dart, her shoulders trembling.

"Far away, back through the forest toward the city," Lucky assured her.

"What if you were followed?" asked Bella. They were the first words that she had spoken to Lucky.

Mickey replied before Lucky could. "We were not followed. The Fierce Dogs had left their camp, and the pups were starving to death. Lucky's right; we could not have left them."

Alpha eyed the pups with wary, narrowed yellow eyes. "They may be small now," he snarled, "but they will grow into Fierce Dogs soon enough. Nasty, wicked creatures."

Wiggle yipped and pressed himself against Lucky's flank as Lick and Grunt watched, their short tails low.

"They don't *have* to grow up that way," Lucky countered. "No dog is *born* vicious. Just like I wasn't *born* streetwise. The Fierce Dogs are taught to be aggressive . . . their lives make them what they are." He looked around the circle of dogs, meeting suspicious expressions. "Alpha, you're half wolf, aren't you? Yet you lead a Pack of dogs." Lucky knew he was treading a dangerous line.

Lick lifted her muzzle to Lucky's ear. "Why don't they like us?" she murmured.

He met her bewildered gaze. "They're confused," he murmured. "They think you're something you're not." He knew this wouldn't make much sense to the pup, but he did not know what else he could say. Mickey had taken a step closer to Grunt, who was still looking defiant despite his lowered tail.

Alpha ignored Mickey and the pups. "What does my bloodline have to do with it?" he rasped. "I may be half wolf but I'm also half dog, and I know how to lead my Pack!"

He took a step forward, and Wiggle yelped and shot beneath Lucky's belly. Lucky spoke quickly. "The Leashed Dogs weren't used to Pack life, but they've learned quickly." He turned to Bruno, making sure his gaze showed mischievous humor when he asked: "Isn't that right?"

The older dog looked away with a murmur of embarrassed agreement.

"Dogs don't really change," said Sweet. "They may pretend to, but that's not the same thing."

Lucky felt his chest tighten. *What does she mean by that?*

"I think they do," said Mickey, taking a step forward so he was standing on one side of the puppies with Lucky on the other. "You remember what I was like. I never thought that I could cope without longpaws. I couldn't imagine a life without them. But now, I *know* they've gone for good. And, I know I *will* survive: I can hunt, and protect myself, and I can contribute to the Pack. Together we're all stronger, aren't we?"

Martha barked in agreement and Snap tilted her head, listening with ears pricked.

"If a Leashed Dog like me can adapt," Mickey continued, "then pups certainly can. Dogs aren't born bad."

"I think that's true," said Moon, shaking her long, silky fur, her eyes on Lick, Wiggle, and Grunt. "Under the Pack's influence, we can teach these puppies how to work gently and effectively together. They don't need to be violent and aggressive like their parents. It's like Lucky said—if the Leashed Dogs have been able to learn wild survival skills, why can't these pups learn to be honorable?"

Alpha's wolfish howl tore over the circle of dogs and Moon shrank back.

"Are you all fools? We *can't* raise Fierce Dogs! It would be like nurturing your own conqueror! We should kill those vermin before they can grow up to attack us. Savagery is in their blood, and sharing our food with them will not change that."

"How can you be so sure?" Lucky barked, bracing his legs defensively as he squared up to the Pack leader.

"*This* is how," snarled Alpha. He jutted out his left foreleg. Lucky saw a deep scar running along the curve of the half wolf's paw, welts of damaged flesh exposed between the strands of shaggy gray fur. He had never noticed it before, but now he shuddered at the sight.

"One of those savage monsters nearly bit it clean off when I was a pup," Alpha growled. "You call them Fierce Dogs, but wolves have a different name for them. To a wolf, they're known as Longpaw Fangs—because the longpaws use them as tools to do their biting for them. And you have the stupidity to lead them into our camp!"

Lucky flinched, a cold shiver of fear passing through him. Looking around him, he met Bella's questioning gaze. *She thinks I've done the wrong thing too. . . .*

Then he remembered how she had let Alpha force him from the Pack, and her foolishness in challenging the Wild Dogs with foxes. His litter-sister was not one to judge any dog's actions.

The dog-wolf wasn't finished. "You say you found the pups on their own?" he snarled. "The Mother-Dog was dead?"

"Yes . . ." Lucky shot a look at Wiggle, who had edged along his flank. Lick stood at her litter-brother's side, with Grunt a pace or two ahead of them, next to Mickey.

"Why would the Fierce Dogs leave the pups behind? What if they come back to collect them and find that they're missing?"

"I wondered that, too," said Mickey. "But their scents had faded and the Mother-Dog had been dead for a full journey of the Sun-Dog, at least."

Alpha gazed over their heads toward the cluster of pine trees. "That means their Pack is out there somewhere, roaming the wild. They could be anywhere. They could be up to *anything.*"

"But that would be true whether the pups were here or not," Martha pointed out in her deep, gentle voice. She padded forward on huge webbed paws. She was easily as large as Alpha, though she was not using her size to command any dog. She lowered her panting, jowly face to the pups. "They're so small," she murmured. "They could grow up to be kind and brave. Who are we to brand them 'bad' dogs when they've barely had a chance at life?"

Lick trotted toward Martha and buried herself beneath the great dog's thick, dark coat. Wiggle scrambled after her, followed by Grunt. Martha nuzzled the pups and they yipped in response, huddling together under her belly.

"They're just pups; we should remember that," said Martha. "And Lucky deserves our trust. He has brought Mickey back to us. We should be grateful that he's here after how he was forced to leave . . ." She looked at Lucky sadly. "Things have changed since the Big Growl, and we're all just trying to figure out how best to survive—it's like Mickey said, we need to stick together." She raised her great furry head to Alpha. "If danger *does* come to the camp, we can beat it as a Pack, and Lucky knows better than any dog how to defend himself."

"The pups should be given a chance," Fiery agreed.

Snap was softening too. "They haven't done anything wrong, have they?"

Alpha turned his head, casting his fierce gaze around the circle of dogs.

He knows he's outnumbered, thought Lucky. *But if he insists that the pups be abandoned or killed, he may still be able to get his way.*

Alpha stared down his long nose at the pups, then raised his head to meet Martha's eye. "Very well," he spat. "They can remain here. . . ." His yellow eyes settled on Lucky. "But they will be *your* responsibility."

"So we can stay with you?" Wiggle yipped, creeping out from beneath Martha's belly to nuzzle Lucky's leg. Martha sighed with relief and Mickey nosed Grunt and Lick protectively.

Lucky never took his eyes off Alpha. "So . . . does that mean . . . ?"

"You will be tolerated for the time being," Alpha barked. "You will return to being Omega—but you will also have the task of training and teaching the Fierce Dog pups, making sure they grow up to become loyal, obedient dogs who can serve the Pack— and not savage monsters who will kill us all while we sleep."

"That will never happen," Lucky promised.

"It's a hard life, being Omega," Whine smirked, his short tail thrashing. "Are you sure you're up to the job, City Dog?"

Lucky swallowed his annoyance. He would suffer the indignity of being Omega if this was Alpha's price for allowing the pups to stay.

The half wolf turned and strode away. Lucky watched him as he made for a knoll covered by spongy green moss and stretched out in the sunshine, rolling onto his side with a yawn.

He was doing his best to save face, but Lucky wondered if his leadership had been dented since the dark cloud after all.

Have the others realized that he is scrabbling for a foothold in this world without longpaws, just like the rest of us?

Lucky turned to the pups, who had gathered between Martha and Mickey.

"Good news," he told them.

"But they don't *want* us," Lick whined.

"They think we're dangerous," Wiggle agreed.

Martha lowered her head and washed them with her tongue. The pups nuzzled against her and Lucky was touched. He saw how they were drawn to her—perhaps she reminded them of their Mother-Dog. Even Grunt yipped happily and nuzzled her leg with his short snout.

"You will be well looked after," Martha assured them. She turned slowly, making for her den, and the pups tumbled after her. He watched them for a moment. Perhaps everything was going to work out after all.

Then his gaze fell on Sweet, who was sitting nearby, washing one elegant paw, a strange expression on her face as she peered at him. Was she sad . . . or angry? Lucky's ears drooped and he cocked his head at her, but the swift-dog looked away, twisting around to groom her tail.

Lucky turned to a nudge from Bella. He hadn't noticed her approaching. Her pink tongue lolled in her panting mouth and she reached forward to lick his nose, but he backed away.

"Don't be like that!" She pawed the ground, then approached again, but he raised his haunches and she stopped in her tracks. "Please, Lucky. I'm so sorry for everything. We haven't even had a chance to talk alone since the dogfight. I *have to* talk to you."

Lucky made as if to leave and she called after him. "What I said to Alpha was true. I was a fool to attack the Wild Pack, and even more of a fool for doing it without warning you."

Lucky raised his muzzle. "And the foxes?"

Bella dropped her head. "That was a terrible mistake. And I should have spoken up for you when Alpha told you to leave the Pack. I really wanted to, but . . . I just *felt* like, more than anything, I had to do my best for the Leashed Dogs. I was scared of what would happen if Alpha attacked us or kicked us out. I didn't know how the Pack would survive. Can you forgive me?"

Lucky felt a tug in his chest. He tried to chase it away with an angry growl. *Bella stayed silent when Alpha cast me out,* he reminded himself. *She let me carry the worst of the blame for the dogfight. She betrayed me! What she did was unforgiveable.*

His tail shot out behind him and he tried to walk away, but he hadn't gone three dog-lengths when she called to him again.

"Yap . . . ?"

Lucky stopped in his tracks. In an instant he was at his Mother-Dog's side, his littermates jostling against him in a jumble of soft bodies. He turned and met Bella's eye. Her long snout was low and she gazed up at him, her eyes large and sad.

Lucky sighed. "I know that you did it for the Pack. Your heart was in the right place. It always is."

"Can you forgive me?" she repeated in a whisper.

"Come here," he replied. She bounded up to him and licked his muzzle, nudging and whining with relief.

I can forgive you, Bella, he thought. *But I can't forget.*

He wanted to trust his litter-sister, but he couldn't—not after everything she had done.

CHAPTER FOURTEEN

Lucky yawned and settled down in the long grass, listening as Mickey told Bella, Daisy, Bruno, and Sunshine about the state of their homes in the crumbling city. Martha was sitting some distance away with the Fierce Dog pups. The rest of the Pack was scattered around, resting before nightfall.

Lucky looked around appreciatively. The camp was every bit as good as Daisy had promised, with its sun-soaked meadow where the dogs had gathered, and a large cave at the edges of the forest where they could sleep in warmth and safety. Deep inside the cave was a nook selected to be the pup den, where Moon nursed Nose and Squirm.

It felt wonderful to be back in the safety of the Pack after the hardships since he had left.

"You wouldn't believe it," Mickey whined. "The city was worse than it had been the last time we were there. All the front yards are wild, and the streets have even more wounds in them—with foul liquid pouring out."

"There was no sign that the longpaws had returned?" asked little Sunshine as she miserably tugged at a burr caught in her filthy white tail. "Not one?"

"They can't have come back," Mickey yowled. "Everything there was stale or wild."

"It's still hard to think of the city without longpaws, even though I've seen it with my own eyes," said Bella.

Mickey sniffed. "There were *some* longpaws—a couple at least."

Bruno pricked up his ears and Daisy jumped to her paws.

"But they were not good ones," Mickey added quickly. "These longpaws were mean and angry. They were the kind that want to hurt dogs."

"The scary ones with the yellow pelts and black faces?" asked Bella.

"No, these longpaws were scraggy and old. They were entering houses and *stealing things*! We defended my house, didn't we, Lucky? I—I mean Omega," the black-and-white dog added.

Lucky gave him a nod. *It's all right. I agreed to be Omega—let Alpha have his rules.*

Mickey's black ears fell as he went on. "But the house was

all broken, and then it caved in. It was horrible. All of you were right—there's nothing for us in the city anymore."

Lucky lifted his muzzle and gazed into the sky. The Sun-Dog was starting his slow descent over the high white clouds. Lucky's head sank back against the moss, his eyes closing. It had been a long few days and it was pleasant just to sit and think.

"So they really have gone for good," said Bruno sadly.

"Well," sighed Sunshine. "We have to do our best to put them completely out of our minds. That is the only way we can survive now."

Lucky opened one eye and looked at her. He was impressed that she, of all the Leashed Dogs, would show such resolve.

Sunshine noticed him looking at her. "Omega," she began nervously. "What made you decide to come back? Oh, I'm so glad you did but . . . I didn't think that you would."

Lucky sighed. "It's like Mickey said, the city is ruined. And then we found the pups. We knew they'd be safer here."

Mickey yipped in acknowledgment.

Sunshine cocked her fluffy white head. "Is that the only reason?"

Lucky was about to admit that he'd missed the Pack when he was distracted by a distant thrumming that reminded him of fluttering bugs he had once seen in trees. His ears pricked up and he raised his snout.

Night insects . . . He looked up at the sky. It was not dark yet. *Why are they out before the Sun-Dog has finished his journey?*

Lucky's thoughts were drowned out by the sound, which was rapidly growing in volume to a deep drone. The dogs raised their heads in unison and Mickey yelped: "It's the giant loudbirds! We saw them in the city!"

Lucky squinted at the sky, fear clenching at his stomach. *What are the loudbirds doing now? Are they still searching for sick longpaws?*

Mickey was right—several of the huge birds were swinging into view, gliding over from the forest. Panic coursed through the Pack. Sunshine and Bruno whimpered and cowered. A short distance away, Alpha and Sweet were on their paws, barking. Mickey was still saying something but one of the birds had dropped overhead and was hovering in the sky, thrashing the air so loudly with its wings that it swallowed his words. Lucky saw Mickey back into Bella. Bella threw up her head and barked. The two dogs stood close as chaos broke out all around them.

The loudbird leaped up high enough for Lucky to catch what the dogs around him were saying.

"Longpaws!" barked Daisy. "There are longpaws trapped inside the birds!"

The dogs fell silent a moment, staring up at the bird. Yellow-furred longpaws were hanging out of the gashes in the bird's flank.

"It's true!" Bruno gasped. "There are longpaws up there trying to escape the belly of that hideous creature!"

"We should help them!" Sunshine howled. Lucky threw her a wary look. Had she already forgotten her promise to put longpaws out of her mind?

"No, Sunshine," Mickey warned. "These longpaws are no friends of dogs! We need to stay back."

Snap had drawn closer, perhaps realizing that Mickey and Lucky had something to say about the giant bird. Dart and Spring followed her and they huddled close to Lucky, waiting for him to speak.

"They aren't trying to escape," Lucky barked, raising his voice as the huge bird swept a loop over their heads. "We saw a bird like this settle in the forest. The longpaws left and returned, which means that they are not prisoners. I think they are controlling the bird somehow."

Alpha and Sweet approached, their eyes fixed to the great bird overhead. They growled and barked as it started to sink over the valley, whipping up a ferocious wind beneath its wings that flattened their fur and shook the pine trees at the edge of the camp.

"It's going to land!" barked Bruno. "Maybe the longpaws will get out, like they did in the forest." He started pawing the ground excitedly. "We should try to find it! We should help the longpaws." The bird was moving back to the deep forest, beyond the cluster of pine trees. Bruno started after it. Lucky saw Alpha's eyes darken. The dog-wolf was about to say something, but Bella got in first.

"No!" she barked, and Bruno stopped in his tracks. "No dog chases the bird!" She turned to each Leashed Dog, giving them a stern look. "That goes for all of you. Don't you remember how the yellow-furred longpaws treated Daisy? They are *not* friendly. I'd never trust a longpaw that covers its face, much less one that chooses to live inside the belly of a loudbird!"

Alpha growled his agreement and Bruno dropped guiltily to the ground, his tail pressed to his flank. Sunshine crouched beside him.

Lucky stood by, his ears pricked. The shiny bird disappeared beyond the pine trees. Eventually its whirring drone became quieter. The branches of the pine trees went on swaying but their trunks grew still. Lucky craned his neck, his body frozen. He could hear the crunch of the longpaws as they ambled heavily over twigs and leaves. Their harsh barks sounded sinister in the silence that followed the bird's descent. Lucky's ears flattened and his stomach clenched.

After a short while, the terrible thrumming began again. The Pack waited tensely, low to the ground. They watched, wide-eyed, as the loudbird rose from the forest floor and swept away beyond a bank of tall trees.

Lucky rose to his paws, his ears pricked and his tail straight behind him. *What can this mean?* he wondered. *What are the longpaws up to?*

Lucky wandered along the edges of the camp, feeling a shiver of loneliness as he looked beyond the rushing water to the thistles on the river's far bank. He shook the feeling away. He had work to do before nightfall—Omega work, gathering bedding for the shelter. He used his snout to shuffle some dried leaves and twigs into a pile, then scooped them up in his jaws and made for the cave. He dropped them at the entrance by the overhanging brambles and retraced his steps to the riverbank. He padded around, sniffing until he found a nice, damp clump of moss. He began digging it up with his paws—it came up easily enough into a wet pile. Once the moss dried out, it would make a comfortable bed to sleep on.

A prouder dog would have said these tasks were beneath him, and even Lucky found himself fighting the impulse to dip his head in shame when he passed Dart and Daisy on patrol.

He trudged back to the shelter with a mouthful of moss. Whine appeared from behind a tangle of nettles, his long tongue lolling from the side of his mouth. "You dropped some, *Omega.*"

Lucky's neck snapped around and he glared at the little dog.

"Just trying to be helpful," Whine yapped. Lucky could see the glint of pleasure in the other dog's eyes. The former Omega was enjoying Lucky's humiliation. Lucky raised his tail and strutted past Whine toward the shelter, his head held high. As he rounded down the slope toward the brambles he almost dropped the moss in surprise—the pile of bedding that he'd gathered had doubled in size. Lucky blinked at it, confused, when little Sunshine scampered up to him and added some leaves.

Lucky dropped the moss and rubbed his paw against his chops, wiping away the bitter aftertaste.

"Sunshine, what are you doing?"

She wagged her tail, turning proudly to the mound of bedding. "Helping, of course. When I was Omega, I did this a couple of times. I figured out where to find the softest leaves. The trick is not to go for the really dry ones; they just crumble when you sit on them. When I was making up the bedding in the shelter, I'd set down the moss first, then soft twigs, then half-dry leaves. You have no idea how comfortable a bed all that makes. It's even better than the soft-hide my longpaws gave me!"

Lucky stared at her, his head cocking. "When *you* were Omega?" he asked.

Sunshine yipped, tidying the pile with careful shunts of her muzzle.

"But I thought Whine . . ."

"No, it was me."

Lucky's head drooped sadly at the thought that poor Sunshine had to take the lowest position in the Pack.

Sunshine raised herself to her full height, jutting out her snout. "Don't look at me like that, Lucky! I don't need your pity. I actually liked being Omega. Bella, Martha, and Daisy were still nice to me, and so was Snap. Anyway, I'm good at all those jobs—you know, the ones most dogs feel they're too noble for." She narrowed her eyes, sniffed the pile, and pulled out an old leaf. "Too crumbly," she murmured. She turned back to Lucky. "My longpaws loved it when I helped them, and I was great at it! Every day I would run to collect the papers that came through the door and I'd bring them to my longpaws. In the evening, I'd bring them their paw-covers."

"Paw-covers?" Lucky had never heard of anything like that.

"Soft pelt covers," said Sunshine, as if it were obvious. "Longpaws have furless paws, you know—they get cold!"

Lucky could not imagine such a thing. "You're really good at this," he told her. "And I appreciate your help. But I don't think Alpha would look kindly on it. . . . I don't want him to think I'm slacking off."

Sunshine nodded. "I understand. It's too bad, though. Will you at least let me help you take the stuff inside?"

Lucky dipped his head and the two dogs carried the bedding beneath the brambles into the cave. Then Sunshine shuffled forward on her short legs and Lucky licked her nose. "You're a good dog, Sunshine," he told her. "I bet you made your longpaws really happy."

"Thank you," she murmured, burying her muzzle against his neck. Then she turned and scampered away to join some of the others in the meadow.

CHAPTER FIFTEEN

"Are you ready?" asked Lucky.

"Ready!" yipped Wiggle. He dived at Lucky, who sprang back, just out of the pup's reach. "I'll get you!" joked Wiggle, charging forward on his thick little legs. This time Lucky let the pup pounce on him and they jostled and sparred. He was surprised at Wiggle's strength. It took some effort to flip him over and pin him down.

"You're a great wrestler," Lucky panted, impressed not only with the pup's strength, but by his speed and technique.

Lick and Grunt watched, their short tails lashing. Lucky glanced up and met Sweet's eyes, narrowed in concentration as she observed the lesson.

Is she here to observe the pups . . . or me? he wondered. Even though this was one of his agreed duties, it wasn't exactly Omega work. Lucky was sure Alpha had sent her to keep an eye on him as much as the three Fierce Dog pups.

Wiggle yipped, struggling to escape Lucky's hold, and Lucky turned his attention back on the wriggling pup. His grip was firm but gentle, careful to avoid Wiggle's throat and belly—the delicate areas.

The pup is growing up fast. Soon he'll be the one who'll have to go easy on me!

If Lucky could teach the pups to be honorable and good-natured, they would certainly be an asset. Who would dare attack a Pack with Fierce Dogs among them?

"Lunge for his neck, Wiggle!" barked Grunt. "If you can't reach, kick with your legs! Imagine you're being attacked by a monster—it's evil and cunning, but you're smarter and faster. Try to find any soft bits of his body, like the neck or the muzzle, and bite as hard as you can!"

Wiggle twisted and thrashed, planting a firm kick on Lucky's chest that winded him, though he didn't release the pup.

"That's no good!" Grunt snarled. "Come on, Wiggle! If the coyotes had caught up with you, you'd be dead by now! Use your teeth!"

Lucky shot Grunt a look, painfully aware of Sweet's eyes on all four of them. "It's not about the damage you can do to your opponent," he said mildly. "It's about protecting yourself and the Pack while keeping your honor. In the first place, fights should always be avoided. But if you *must* fight, the focus should be on defense, not uncontrolled aggression." He looked down at Wiggle, who was bucking and bending in frustration. "Wiggle is in a dangerous position right now, but he can protect himself, even on his back. Like this. . . ." Lucky dropped onto Wiggle and flipped him around so the pup was on top; then he wrapped his paws around Wiggle's head, forcing his snout to the ground. Wiggle snarled and Lucky spoke over him: "You see? The worst injuries you can suffer from another dog are inflicted by the teeth, and this maneuver will limit your opponent's ability to bite. By gripping Wiggle's head, I've stopped him from taking a chunk out of me!

"Now try it again, Wiggle." Lucky released his grip and the pup struggled to his paws. Wiggle shook himself off with an angry yip.

"You're doing really well," Lucky added, licking the pup on the head. Wiggle dropped to the ground and rolled onto his back. Lucky planted his paws on the pup's chest. "Try to wrap your paws around my neck and pull my head down."

Wiggle reached out, his paws scrambling at Lucky's neck, but his forelegs were too short for him to get a proper grip. He strained and grunted, his paws thrashing, but Lucky twisted out of reach and shook himself free.

The pup growled in frustration as he sank to the ground. "It's impossible!"

"No, you'll get it," started Lucky, but Grunt brushed past him. "Don't give up!" he told Wiggle. "You need to be determined, whatever the enemy holds over you. Next time, you will beat him!"

Wiggle lifted his head and allowed Grunt to lick his nose. Lucky watched, admiring Grunt's loyalty to his litter-brother. *The pup is a natural leader. With a little patience and compassion, he could be a great asset to the Pack. I just hope Sweet can see what I see.*

"Let's try again," said Lucky.

Wiggle spun around and charged at him, catching him off guard. The pup pummeled Lucky's muzzle with his paws and when Lucky ducked, he clung on to his back and buried his teeth in Lucky's flesh. A blast of pain shot through Lucky's neck and he shook Wiggle off with a yelp. Sweet growled low in her throat and tensed, but didn't move. Across the clearing, Bella looked up from grooming herself and narrowed her eyes.

Wiggle fell back, shocked by Lucky's cry. "I'm sorry," he whined, dipping his head, his tail drooping. "I shouldn't have been so rough."

Lucky had been nipped in play-fights, but never like this. The pain still surged at his neck but he tried not to show it.

Wiggle didn't mean to hurt me—he just doesn't know his own strength. And it felt like his fangs are starting to come through. . . .

"I'm fine," Lucky murmured, giving Wiggle's ears an affectionate lick. He beckoned the pup's littermates to come nearer. They sat in front of him. Lucky spoke softly, but he was sure to make his voice loud enough for Sweet to hear. "As you get older, you will develop fangs. They're going to be very important for you; they will help you catch prey, and to defend yourself against an attack. But they can also cause great damage if you're careless. Can I trust you to be careful when you play with one another or other dogs? Remember not to bite too hard."

Lick and Wiggle yipped their agreement and, after a moment, Grunt gave a nod.

"Good," said Lucky. "Once all your fangs have come through, it'll be time for you to choose your proper dog names."

"Really?" yipped Wiggle.

"Yes. Every Wild Dog I've ever met has chosen their name when they grew up. Leashed Dogs are named by their longpaws." Lucky shook himself. It wasn't an entirely good memory for him— the longpaws he had lived with as a pup had never cared for him the way the Leashed Dogs' longpaws did.

"Anyway, you'll be all grown up soon enough," said Lucky, surprised to feel a bite of sadness in his belly.

Martha appeared from the edge of the camp, padding languidly on her webbed paws. The pups pounced and yipped in excitement, bounding toward her and nuzzling her legs. She greeted them by licking their ears and turned to Lucky.

"I thought I might take these youngsters off your paws for a while. I'm going on patrol with Moon and her pups; maybe Lick, Grunt, and Wiggle would like to help? Only the cleverest dogs with the finest senses are invited to go on patrol."

The pups started running in excited circles.

"Yes, please!" yapped Lick.

"We'll be the best at patrolling!" added Grunt. "No dog has senses as good as ours!"

Lucky was touched by their enthusiasm. "What a good idea," he said. He sat down to wash his paws as Martha went to join Moon, the pups bouncing and scampering at her side. His neck still stung where Wiggle had bitten it, but he did not think it was bleeding.

He looked up at Sweet, but as he did she turned and padded away, her face unreadable. Lucky felt a pang of sadness as he watched her go. Couldn't she even bear to speak to him now? Perhaps Beta shouldn't be seen discussing Pack business with Omega. He hoped she wouldn't make too much of Wiggle's mistake when she reported to Alpha.

On the other side of the camp, Bella stood up and padded toward him, throwing a look at the big water-dog as she and the puppies rounded behind the pine trees and disappeared from view.

"I saw what that pup did. It looked painful," she said. She leaned over to inspect the bite, but he pulled away from her. The swift movement sent a shot of pain through Lucky's neck and he struggled not to wince or yelp.

"He was only playing," said Lucky defensively. "He didn't mean anything by it."

Bella whined uncertainly. "He can already cause damage and he's only a play-fighting *pup*. What will happen when he and the others have deadly weapons in their mouths? Don't you remember the Dog-Garden?" She shuddered, her ears twitching.

"They're still young, Bella. We can raise them in the right way. We can *teach* them to be careful. Just because they're Fierce Dogs, that doesn't mean—"

A howl cut through his words, immediately followed by a volley of distressed barks. Lucky's heart lurched. He bolted toward the river with Bella at his side, in the direction of the sounds. Other dogs had also heard and were tearing across the camp. Lucky saw the flash of Mickey's black-and-white pelt and the patchwork of Dart's mottled coat. By the time he and Bella reached the riverbank, half of the Pack was already there, although Alpha was not among them.

Lucky could hardly believe his eyes—gentle Martha was facing off against Moon, spit frothing at her jowly lips. The Fierce Dog pups were lined up behind her, Lick and Wiggle looking tense and fearful, while Grunt snarled and gnashed his teeth. Lucky saw that he had short white fangs, just like Wiggle's.

Hostile scents tingled Lucky's nose. He had never seen Martha like this and it disturbed him. And where were Moon's pups? He could smell them; they had to be close.

Bella, Mickey, and the other dogs were still as they watched the standoff.

"They're little savages!" Moon growled. "Look what that one did to her!" She glared accusingly at Grunt.

Lucky crept around Martha and Moon. He spotted Squirm crouching by a tawny bush. She whimpered pathetically as her litter-brother, Nose, nuzzled her, his eyes leaping fretfully to the Fierce Dog pups.

Lucky's stomach churned with nerves. "What happened?"

Moon turned her eyes on him. "That vicious little Grunt attacked my Squirm for no reason at all!"

"They were play-fighting," snapped Martha. "It just got out of hand—it happens sometimes. Grunt didn't mean any harm." Then she gave a shake of her shaggy head and sighed deeply. Her face softened and she lowered her body so she no longer towered over the Mother-Dog. "Let's not allow this to become a reason to fight, Moon. Little Grunt has learned his lesson."

Moon looked at Martha uncertainly a moment. Then she slowly lowered her hackles. Lucky was relieved when the two dogs nosed each other and Moon turned back to Squirm, who was not badly injured. It was a good thing that Fiery was out somewhere, presumably with Alpha and Sweet. Lucky didn't want to think about what the great brown dog might have done to Grunt.

Lick and Wiggle pawed at Martha, who lowered her head to comfort them. Only Grunt remained alone, a scowl darkening his face as he watched Moon beckon her puppies away.

Lucky stood by, barely feeling the bite throbbing at his neck now. He cared about the pups; he was also well aware that he had brought them into the camp. He would be blamed if anything went wrong.

Another clash like that and they'd all be out of the Pack for good.

The pups are going to need a lot more teaching, he thought. *Grunt most of all.*

Lucky sighed and plodded through the forest toward the river. The bedding in the hunters' den needed to be changed. It seemed as though one of the worst parts of being Omega was going to be the boredom—repeating the same tasks over and over again, never getting to take part in the thrill of a hunt or even the responsibility of patrolling the camp border.

The riverbank was the best spot for digging up nice, soft moss. Lucky sidled up to the bank and started sniffing his way through tangles of grass, where tall trees closed in again, marking the edge of the forest. He ducked under them, spotting some decent leaves—only half-dry, as Sunshine had recommended—and was scooping them up when he heard a twig snap beneath a paw. Turning, he saw Bruno making his way under a huge oak. The old dog had risen to the position of hunter while Lucky and

Mickey were away. Lucky guessed he was sniffing around for prey. The other hunters must be in the forest too, but he couldn't scent any of them nearby.

Lucky dropped the mouthful of leaves and pressed deeper into the forest, but Bruno called after him.

Lucky's fur bristled. He kept walking, almost at a trot. "I have to gather leaves before no-sun," he barked over his shoulder. He could hear Bruno behind him, treading with clumsy steps. Lucky knew that the old dog would struggle to keep up with him.

How did he get to be a hunter? I can't imagine he's caught much prey, thought Lucky. He quickened his pace. *Can't he just leave me alone? Like it isn't bad enough being Omega; he has to rub my nose in it!*

"Lucky! Slow down!" Bruno was wheezing.

Lucky paused, his fur itching as he pawed the ground. A few days of being called Omega had been enough for it to stop stinging—but now he almost resented Bruno using his real name. *You wouldn't call me Lucky if Alpha were nearby. . . .*

"It's so hard, hunting out here," Bruno whined. "Fiery decided we should split up to sniff out small prey, but I've been searching for ages and I haven't caught so much as a mouse."

Lucky grunted, looking back over his shoulder, but instead of meeting Bruno's eye he scanned the surrounding forest. It was growing dark. He would have to hurry up with the bedding to avoid giving Alpha something to hold against him. From the corner of his eye, he saw Bruno dip his head.

"I'm sorry, Lucky," he said. "I should never have helped trap you like that. I honestly don't know what came over me. I don't blame you for being angry."

The older dog sounded so forlorn that Lucky felt a stab of pity. Then he remembered how Bruno had thrown him down at Alpha's command.

If the black cloud had not appeared, I would have been scarred forever!

Lucky turned on Bruno angrily. "What were you thinking? You acted like a fox, or a sharpclaw. Sneaking up and attacking like that is not a dog's style. Where's your sense of honor? And after everything we've been through!"

Bruno's nose sank to the forest floor. "You're right," he whimpered. "I'm so sorry. I was scared . . . scared of Alpha and the whole situation. I couldn't believe what happened with the foxes—everything got out of control so quickly. I thought being part of a Pack would make me feel safe. . . ." His ears drooped. "Lucky, do you remember when I drank the bad water and got sick?"

"Of course I remember!" snapped Lucky. "It was me who saved you. Do you remember *that*, Bruno?"

The other dog flopped onto his belly with a whimper. "I do. And I haven't forgotten. My point is, I didn't know water could hurt you. Even things that used to be harmless have been turned dangerous by the Big Growl. I thought I was coping with all the changes, adapting to life in the Leashed Pack. But . . ." He trailed off in a pitiful whine. Lucky could see this wasn't easy for him.

Bruno took a deep breath. "The truth is that my fears got the better of me. I never used to be scared of anything. I was the toughest dog on the street! Now I can't sleep at night for fear that a fight will break out in the Pack. Even the light of the Sun-Dog doesn't make me feel safe. You never know what's out there, what's watching from behind the branches. Now I'm scared of everything."

Bruno's eyes flicked across the trees and he started to shiver, even though it wasn't cold. "I guess I wanted to fit in. When Alpha asked for help . . . I didn't think to refuse. There was something about him that just made me want to do whatever he said, for the good of the Pack. He promoted me to hunter after you'd gone— said a loyal, tough dog like me was wasted on patrol. I should've been celebrating, but every time I've gone out to catch prey I've just felt guilty." He gazed down his snout, as though talking to the earth. "Please, Lucky. You know I'm not a bad dog, really."

Lucky turned to face Bruno, his anger melting away. "I know you're not," he said.

Bruno looked up at him with big, sad eyes. His bushy tail gave a hesitant thump. "You forgive me?"

Lucky sighed. "I guess so. . . ."

Bruno climbed to his paws. He panted happily, his tail beating the air.

Lucky relaxed his stance, but inside he felt a wrinkle of unease. He gazed up at the branches overhead.

If even kind dogs like Bruno can turn on their friends, what hope does the Pack have of nurturing Fierce Dog pups?

He shook himself. "Do you need help hunting?"

Bruno's tail thrashed happily. "I thought you'd never ask!" he yelped, approaching shyly but falling short of touching noses.

"You realize that I'm the Omega?" said Lucky, throwing him a sideways look.

"That's just a title," said Bruno quickly. "That's not who you *are*. I know what you're capable of, Lucky."

Lucky lifted his muzzle and took a deep sniff. He could smell the damp earth, the clean river water, the heat of dogs back at the shelter, even the hint of pine trees on the other side of the camp. There were small animals too, but none close enough to catch.

"Come on," Lucky said. "Let's go searching."

The two of them strayed farther into the forest. Soon Lucky picked up the scent of prey. He dropped his snout, nosing through a pile of fallen leaves and identifying some tracks.

Bruno sidled up to him. "Lucky, do you think that scent is . . . a bit strange?"

Lucky sniffed again, catching something flinty in the soil. The fur prickled along his neck and he swallowed. "There *is* something weird about it, although I can't figure out what it is." He looked around. The shadows were lengthening between the trees. "Still, food is food, and soon it'll be too dark to see."

A bird trilled overhead and Bruno's body stiffened. Lucky started padding between the trees again, hearing Bruno hurrying after him. They edged around a tangle of brambles and up a little ridge, where Lucky caught the warm, sweet scent of small animals. He looked to Bruno, who gave a sharp nod—he had smelled it too.

As one, the dogs lowered their haunches and stalked low to the ground. They eased themselves over a clutch of vines past the broken trunk of a fallen tree. The scent of the animals grew stronger.

Birds . . . but don't they all nest in branches? Why are they grouping together on the forest floor?

Lucky paused. "They aren't moving. Maybe they're hurt, or . . ." He sniffed again. Now he sensed it—the death scent. A prickle of fear caught the back of his neck, but Bruno had already pushed on ahead of him, hurrying around the fallen trunk with an excited yip.

"Pigeons! Two of them!"

Lucky approached more warily. The gray-feathered birds were limp, their small eyes glinting, their beaks slightly parted. Lucky held back, watching the darkening woods and listening for movement. "They only died a short time ago. . . ."

"That means they're fresh," said Bruno, licking his chops.

Lucky gave an uneasy whimper. "It also means that whoever killed them could still be close."

"I don't smell anyone," said Bruno with a dismissive wag of the tail. "Come on, let's get them back to camp."

Lucky could not smell anyone either, but he stood warily, reluctant to touch the dead birds. He could feel the fur on his spine standing up. "I don't know, Bruno . . . I don't feel right about this. Whoever killed these birds will be back for them—and they will probably be back very soon. They could track us back to the camp. There are pups there—"

"There's also Alpha, Sweet, Fiery, and all the others. I'd like to see them try!" He gathered one of the pigeons in his jaws and turned in the direction of their camp. Lucky paused, his ears pricked. Was that a twig snapping, deeper in the forest? He tried to ignore the heavy tread of Bruno's paws as he listened.

Nothing.

All that talk of danger . . . it must be getting to me.

Lucky shook himself, then scooped up the remaining bird and followed Bruno.

As Lucky loped out of the forest and arrived at the camp with Bruno by his side, he saw Sweet treading toward them. His heart gave a small tremor of excitement—was the swift-dog finally going to talk to him? His tail twitched and he cocked his head, but Sweet did not return the gestures as she stopped a short distance from Lucky.

"Omega, Alpha wants to speak to you," she barked. Before Lucky could reply, she turned and entered the shelter. Lucky guessed he was supposed to follow her.

"I can take the kill," Bruno offered.

Lucky gave a nod, dropping the limp bird so that Bruno could scoop it up with the other one that he carried. As Omega, Lucky was not supposed to be hunting, and it would be wrong for him to approach the shelter with the bird in his jaws.

Sweet was already inside when Lucky dipped his head beneath the brambles and entered the dim light of the cave. She strode to Alpha's corner—the warmest and farthest from the entrance—and stood next to the half wolf. He was stretched out on his bed of moss and leaves, collected by Lucky as part of his duties as Omega. Alpha rose to his paws as Lucky came closer, throwing back his head in a gaping yawn that revealed his huge, pointed fangs. Lucky's stomach tightened as other dogs approached, watching with interest. Fiery and Moon were both there, as was Martha, though there was no sign of any of the pups. Looking over the dogs, Lucky noticed that Spring was nowhere to be seen—she must be watching the pups deep inside the cave.

Alpha had stopped yawning and was staring ahead as Lucky approached.

What does he want? I've done my best to play by his rules, to be an obedient Omega. Is he going to cast me out of the Pack after all?

Lucky caught Bella watching him, her muzzle tight with tension. She must have been thinking the same thing.

The half wolf spoke in his strange, deep voice. "You may be wondering why I called you here, Omega."

Lucky's fur bristled but he stayed silent.

"Despite your lowly status I will you do you the favor of discussing a serious matter *with* you, since you were the one who brought the problem into my camp."

Lucky instantly thought of the pups, and the confrontation between Moon and Martha. He glanced at the water-dog, who returned his look with a worried expression in her eyes.

Lucky turned back to Alpha and made an effort to keep his voice even. "What do you mean?"

"Those little Fierce Dogs of yours attacked Moon's pups. There are witnesses. We need to make a decision about whether we should be harboring potential enemies—particularly those that were brought here after the black Sky-Dog appeared in warning."

Standing by Alpha's side, Sweet and Moon barked in support. Lucky felt his heartbeat quicken. What had happened while he had been in the forest? How had a simple case of play-fighting getting out of hand turned into this?

"If a pup can attack another pup without any reason," Fiery growled, his lips curling back in anger, "what will he do once he's a full-grown Fierce Dog?"

"The black cloud was an omen!" Dart put in. "Don't you remember that awful day? The sky screamed, and then it came! And soon after that, *they* came!"

There was a bark of agreement from Moon.

Alpha raised his muzzle and the other dogs fell silent. "I was willing to give the three pups a chance despite my reservations, but they are showing all the violence and anger we have come to expect of their kind. Soon they will cause real damage. It will not be long before their fangs are long and their bodies powerful— every dog here will be at risk."

"Sorry, Alpha, but I think that's unfair." It was Martha. "It's true; the pups are strong, but they will learn how to control them- selves in time. They are not cruel or violent by nature—and they are all very sorry about what happened."

Bella barked in agreement but Lucky was quiet.

What Martha said is true of Wiggle and Lick, he thought, *but what about Grunt?* He remembered the pup's expression during the confron- tation between Martha and Moon. He had not looked sorry. . . .

Lucky shook himself. It wasn't fair to be hard on the pup—not after everything he had been through. *Grunt's first experience in this world was the death of his Mother-Dog. The very first feelings he felt were grief and anger that he could not explain. There is still time for him to learn how to handle his emotions. He does not have to grow up into a bad dog.*

Alpha stretched his long forelegs. "We have to find out the

truth of their natures. We need to be *sure* that the pups won't grow up to tear us all to shreds in our sleep."

Most of the Pack growled their agreement at this—even Leashed Dogs like Daisy and Sunshine.

"All dogs have the ability to be aggressive when they think their lives are in danger," Lucky said. "Hasn't every dog in this Pack gone to great lengths to ensure their own survival?"

"Survival is one thing," Alpha snarled. "Outright savagery is another. Perhaps all dogs have an inner fighter, even feeble ones." He cast a disdainful look at Whine, who cowered and looked away. "Fierce Dogs are different—they *enjoy* destroying their enemies." The dog-wolf licked the scar on his forepaw, then raised his eyes to stare hard at Lucky. "I have to find out if these angry little pups will be loyal and obedient to their new Pack. We have a right to know the truth about them while they're still small enough to be *dealt* with."

A shiver ran along Lucky's spine. He was about to protest, but Martha spoke first.

"What exactly do you mean by 'dealt with'?" she snarled.

The half wolf's hackles rose and his pale eyes bore into her until she looked away, lowering her head. When he spoke again there was a note of finality in his voice. "First the pups must be tested. Then I will decide what's to be done." He sank onto his bed of moss and leaves and turned his face away. The dogs took their cue to disperse.

Martha padded away, grumbling about the decision as Mickey sought to console her. Lucky walked behind Sweet. Once they were out of Alpha's earshot, he murmured to her: "Do you support this?"

She didn't turn to look at him. "Alpha gets to make the decisions. That's why he's Alpha."

Lucky thought about this. *How did Alpha get to his position?* he wondered. *Does it have to be the fiercest dog who gets to be leader of a Pack? Could a quieter, gentler dog rise to be Alpha?*

Sweet licked her paw impatiently. Lucky was reminded that nothing had changed—she still had not forgiven him. He growled in frustration. "It's not right to treat the pups like this. Their Mother-Dog died, then their Pack abandoned them—they have suffered enough! Isn't it any wonder that, after all that, they would be a bit more aggressive than is in their nature? They can *change*."

"They're dishonorable little runts," Sweet growled with a dismissive toss of her sleek head. Then she looked right at Lucky. "They can't be *trusted*."

The swift-dog started to walk away. Lucky felt the blood drain from his body.

"Please, Sweet," he yelped. "Testing the pups will be unfair. And you *know* that the dogs can change—you've done it yourself! You are now a tough dog, with status in this large Pack. But you were not *always* tough—remember?"

Sweet stopped in her tracks, her head snapping around to look at him. Her lip curled defensively. "What do you mean by that, *Omega?*"

Lucky was shocked. "Call me whatever name you like . . . *Beta*," he snarled. "At least I'm not a coward! It was not *me* who was scared of a dead longpaw, was it? You may be impressed with yourself now, but back in the city you were a different dog . . . you were terrified, helpless . . . *pathetic.*"

Her eyes blazed with anger. Lucky wanted to take back the words as soon as he had barked them. She may have ignored him and mocked him, but that did not stop him from feeling like he had gone too far.

He was surprised when the fierce look on Sweet's face faded. "I suppose you have a point, though you didn't have to make it in such a nasty way."

"I know; I was just frustrated. I shouldn't have—"

She dismissed his words with a jerk of her head. "Let's leave it at that." She glanced back toward the dog-wolf's corner of the shelter. "Alpha has a point too, you know? Fierce Dogs *are* enemies of ours. It makes sense to find out for sure if these pups are beyond the help of the Pack. It could save all our lives."

CHAPTER SIXTEEN

As the Sun-Dog bounded beyond the trees, the Pack gathered to eat the prey the hunters had brought back for them. Alpha stepped forward first, salivating, and clamped his wolfish jaws down on the largest rabbit in the pile.

Lucky lay down in the grass and groomed his paws. The role of Omega had taught him the value of patience—or at least that there was no point watching and drooling while every other dog in the Pack ate their fill, worrying about how much would be left for him.

Sweet followed Alpha. Moon had lost her right to eat early when she'd stopped nursing, but the weaned pups had taken her place. Nose and Squirm tumbled and play-fought over a mouse before running back to Moon's side to share their spoils. Sunshine had explained to Lucky that they would eat after Alpha and Beta until they were grown enough to choose their new names;

then they'd have to work their way up the Pack ranks like any other dog.

Grunt, Lick, and Wiggle bounded up to the prey pile next, with Martha standing strong behind them. She leaned down and muttered into Lick's ear.

"Not too much now, remember? Eat your fill, but don't be greedy. Make sure your litter-brothers remember too."

The female pup nodded. Sure enough, when she saw Wiggle reaching for a second vole, she gently barged him with her shoulder.

"Greedy guts," she muttered. Wiggle reluctantly put the vole down.

The Hunter Dogs ate next, led by Fiery, and then the Patrol Dogs. Whine tucked in with his usual abandon, as if he was trying to leave as little as possible for Sunshine and Lucky, the only two dogs lower in the Pack than he was. Lucky hid his annoyance with a yawn. He couldn't let Whine see that being Omega was getting to him.

By the time Lucky was allowed to eat, the prey pile was almost gone. He swallowed down a last bite of rabbit and a tiny bird that had already been dead when Bruno had found it.

There was no Great Howl tonight—the Moon-Dog's face was

only a dim sliver in the sky. The dogs scattered as they headed for their dens. In the Patrol Dogs' den, Moon stretched out her legs, forcing Whine to curl up in a dim, damp corner. Lucky saw Bruno sniffing the bedding in the hunters' den and then panting gratefully across the camp at him. Grunt, Lick, and Wiggle were nestled alongside Martha in the open section of the cave, while Moon and Fiery watched over Nose and Squirm in the pup den.

Lucky shivered in his Omega place near the cave's entrance. He turned restlessly, thinking about the Fierce Dog pups. *It's not fair to test them, they're so young. . . .* He spotted Sweet's lean silhouette as she trod lightly between the sleeping dogs. She stood over Lucky, waiting for him to get up and follow her. His stomach tightened.

What did his Beta want in the middle of the night?

He climbed soundlessly to his paws and padded after Sweet. She walked to the far side of the cave, where Daisy was curled up beside Sunshine. Lucky watched, his stomach churning, as Sweet tapped Daisy on the nose.

Why is she waking Daisy? he wondered.

Daisy opened her eyes and blinked at Sweet. Her worried glance drifted to Lucky.

"Come with me," Sweet murmured.

The little dog yawned, then struggled to her paws. "What's going on?" she asked.

"I'll explain when we're outside," Sweet replied, leading Lucky and Daisy past Bella, who stood sentry at the entrance. Bella eyed them curiously but turned away as they stepped out of the cave.

There was a bite in the air. The Sky-Dogs were at rest, the Moon-Dog floating alone in a cloudless no-sun sky. A breeze lifted over the surrounding trees and brushed back the fur on Lucky's throat. Daisy shivered and looked up at Sweet and Lucky.

"What's going on?" asked Daisy, bewildered. She looked from Sweet to Lucky, her ears twitching anxiously.

"I was about to ask Sweet the same thing," said Lucky. "Is this about the pups again?"

"How did you guess?" Alpha's husky voice seemed to float out of the darkness and Lucky's fur rose along his back. A moment later, he spotted the half wolf's shaggy outline as he slunk closer, his yellow eyes glinting in the moonlight.

Daisy took a nervous step toward Lucky.

Lucky thought of the Fierce Dog pups sleeping peacefully with Martha. His chest tightened and his throat felt dry. "You're not going to 'test' them now?" As soon as the words were out, he realized he sounded more hostile than he had intended.

"Not now," snarled Alpha. "At dawn." He turned to Sweet, greeting her with a tap of the nose. He turned back to Lucky. "I went exploring today with Beta and Fiery. Beyond the cave and the forest, there is a ridge of white rock. I want to know what comes after that. Are there other dogs out there? Is there decent prey? Does the river stay clean beyond the ridge?"

Lucky listened uneasily. *Is he planning to send me there right now, in the middle of the night? And why has he called on Daisy?*

As if reading his thoughts, Alpha looked down at Daisy, acknowledging her for the first time. "You will take the Fierce Dog pups."

"Take them . . . ?" Daisy was wide-eyed.

"Through the forest. We need to know that the pups are loyal. That they will obey adult members of the Pack, regardless of how . . ." Alpha paused. He stared down at Daisy. She took a step back, unable to meet his eye.

Lucky's stomach clenched and he swallowed a whine. "You can't use Daisy like that—it isn't fair to her or the pups. A journey through the forest will endanger all their lives."

"It is *necessary*," snapped Alpha. "Daisy will lead the pups to the white ridge, searching for possible new camps. She will find out what is beyond the ridge, and she will return with the pups and report to us what she has seen. Then we will know if those three little brutes can take orders."

Lucky was horrified. By testing the pups, Alpha was putting Daisy in serious danger. Daisy was one of the dogs who the pups could overwhelm, if the urge took them.

"It is not safe in the deep forest without a Pack!" he protested, thinking of the sly coyotes prowling around at night. Catching Daisy's terrified expression, he decided not to mention them. "We don't know what's out there."

"You're not the only dog who can survive alone," snarled Alpha dismissively. "Daisy will have to take care of herself."

Lucky thought about Lick, Grunt, and Wiggle fast asleep at Martha's side. His body tensed protectively. "What about the pups?"

Daisy was trembling. Her eyes shot to the high trees beyond the camp that marked the reappearance of the forest. She looked up at Sweet. "Beta?" she said.

"Yes, Daisy," said Sweet, her voice a level growl. "You will do this, for the good of the Pack. You will leave tomorrow at sunup."

Lucky and Alpha trod over the dewy grass of the meadow to the edges of the forest. Upwind, a dozen long-strides away, Daisy was leading Lick, Grunt, and Wiggle on a path between the trees. Lucky could hear the excited chatter of the pups. It was not long after sunup, and they hadn't journeyed far enough to get tired and cranky just yet.

But how long will this last? Lucky wondered.

"Why were we picked to go on this journey?" Lick was asking.

Lucky had wondered the same thing when Alpha had woken him with a rough nip at his shoulder.

"Get up, Omega, and come with me." When Lucky had given him a blank look, Alpha had gone on in a low growl. "I will be observing the Fierce Dogs from a distance. I want to see for myself how and when they fail our test, and I want you to see it too."

Lucky had suppressed a growl of annoyance and followed Alpha, trailing behind Daisy and the pups as they left the camp.

"Alpha chose you because you're small but strong, like me," Daisy told Lick. "We'll cover a good distance through the forest, but no one will notice us."

"We're going on an adventure!" yipped Wiggle.

"It's about time we were given a *proper* task," said Grunt. Lucky could not see his face but he could hear the satisfied note in the pup's voice. He felt a surge of confidence. *Perhaps this is what he's needed all along—a sense of purpose.*

Lucky and Alpha walked in silence, holding back regularly behind the cover of trees, careful not to get too close to Daisy and the pups, whose progress was slow. The forest cut a sharp course uphill. The land was sandy, making it difficult to climb, and thorny brambles twisted and crawled along the forest floor.

This journey was not going to be easy for the pups.

Lucky heard Daisy instructing the pups. "There's a steep hillock coming up," she told them. "It might be tricky to climb. Take small, careful steps—don't overstretch yourselves, or you may catch on a thorn—or roll backward. Watch me."

Alpha met Lucky's eye with a hard gaze. He could guess what the half wolf was thinking. *This is the first test.*

Lick followed Daisy up the hillock in front of her litter-brothers. She seemed calm and composed, taking small steps as she had been told. Lucky's tail wagged with pride. *She's learned her lesson from the accident with the tree.* He watched as Lick mounted the incline and joined Daisy at the top. The pup gave a yap of delight and shook out her fur.

Wiggle bounded after her, trying to keep pace, but scrambled and slipped on the crumbling earth and slid back down, trying several times to bound up again, only to lose his paws again.

"Small steps, Wiggle," Daisy reminded him.

The little pup gave a determined bark and started to mount the incline again. This time he followed instructions, taking small, careful steps. "Look, I'm climbing it!" he yipped. Soon he was at the top, panting alongside his litter-sister, his stubby tail wagging.

"Remember what I told you, Grunt," said Daisy as the biggest pup started to work his way up the hill.

"I know how to do this," snarled Grunt defensively. He rushed up the steep hillock, his muscular back legs working as he took long, energetic steps. Lucky watched, impressed by the pup's ability. A moment later, Grunt lost his paws and slipped back down to the base of the hillock, dirt-dust billowing around him. The pup sneezed and shook off his fur. Then he stiffened and tried again, running at the hillock, reaching about halfway before sliding down again.

Back at the bottom, he barked: "This is stupid! We left a large, sheltered camp with a big house and porch and everything we could ever need for an empty old hill where the only thing to do is walk. It makes no sense!"

"You're a Wild Dog now," said Daisy firmly as Lick and Wiggle stood by her side. "Sometimes we need to do things for the Pack, like check the forest for new camps. In the future you will hunt or patrol with the Wild Dogs as well. You'll come to love being part of it all."

"We already *have* a Pack," snarled Grunt.

Standing some distance away behind the trunk of an old oak, Alpha turned his cool eyes on Lucky.

He's so sure he's going to be proven right—that the Fierce Dog pups can't be educated. Lucky looked away from Alpha to keep an eye on Grunt.

The pup started mounting the incline again, taking small steps. His quick pace sent clouds of dry earth behind him, and he soon reached the top of the hillock.

Lucky and Alpha walked in silence, keeping a slow pace upwind of Daisy and the pups. Lucky sniffed the air, enjoying the rich scent of earth, pine, and grass. Then he froze: He could smell something else, tangy and familiar—the scent of a dog. Lucky suddenly realized that it was the same odor he had detected on the dead pigeons that he and Bruno had found in the forest near the camp. He glanced at Alpha, who seemed not to have noticed.

A few paces on, Lucky spotted the remains of a small creature. He tapped it with his paw and lowered his muzzle to take a sniff.

"Mouse," said Alpha. He stopped to stretch, showing off his long, muscular limbs.

Lucky caught a trace of that tangy smell. "It was killed by a dog," he told Alpha.

"I know," replied the half wolf indifferently. "It was Twitch."

"Twitch?" Lucky echoed. He looked up, his eyes trailing over tree trunks and a low bush. He remembered the pathetic, injured dog he'd seen while making his way to the city—the dog who'd limped through the forest. *How could a dog like that hunt? How could he survive?*

Alpha stared down his nose at Lucky. "You seem surprised. Do you think it's so hard? That only a City Dog can manage without a Pack? Twitch was always self-reliant. He got along fine, despite his injury. Perhaps because of it."

Lucky's tail gave a wag at this. He had assumed that Twitch wouldn't make it, and he was pleased to know the injured dog was surviving on his own. He watched Alpha from the corner of his eye. He had not imagined that the half wolf would ever stand up for another dog. Perhaps there was something gentler beneath that pelt of gray fur.

"Maybe he's thinking of returning to the Pack," Lucky wondered aloud.

Alpha rose to his full height, glaring out into the forest, but he spoke quite calmly. "He deserted us as a coward—he would not be welcomed back." He turned his wolfish face to Lucky. "And if I catch him hunting in our territory, I'll have him killed."

* * *

Beyond the hillock was a plateau from which it was possible to see the white ridge looming in the distance. There were trees up here but the cover was sparser, with skinny pines replacing the thicker-trunked hardwoods. The terrain was rocky. It would be unforgiving for small, delicate paws.

Lucky and Alpha crouched behind a boulder, within earshot of Daisy and the pups. As the Sun-Dog bounded over the sky, Lucky pitied the three young dogs—they would surely be tired and hungry by now. Their coats gleamed under the gaze of the Sun-Dog and they panted breathlessly. But they persevered, trotting slowly behind Daisy.

"Are we almost there?" yipped Wiggle.

"We'll go a little farther; I can smell water," Daisy told him.

Lick turned to her. "Water? I'm so thirsty! Where is the water?"

"It isn't possible to *smell* water," growled Grunt.

Daisy stopped. "If you take a very deep sniff, you'll be able to smell it too." She crouched down, rested her muzzle on the rocky ground, and took a long breath.

Lick and Wiggle mirrored Daisy's movements, lowering themselves onto the ground. Lucky tensed, wondering what

Grunt would do. He watched Alpha from the corner of his eye. The dog-wolf was also observing the exchange. *Please, Grunt, don't challenge Daisy's authority,* Lucky silently willed.

Grunt looked skeptical, but he dipped his head and sniffed. For a moment he hardly moved. Then his tail leaped up behind him.

"Water!" he barked. "Not far away! I *can* smell it!"

"I can, too!" yipped Lick. She bounded up to Grunt and they tumbled on the ground, rolling and barking. Then they raced off in the direction of the water.

"Not too fast," Daisy called after them, but her tone was cheerful and she started after them with her tail thrashing.

Only little Wiggle stayed where he was. "I can't smell anything," he whined.

Daisy skidded on her paws. She returned to the pup and licked his ear comfortingly. "Keep trying," she told him. "You will."

The little stream cleaved a shaft of gray rock that cut through the pines. Daisy and the pups drank thirstily and washed their paws. Then Daisy led them toward the white ridge.

She wants to be far enough away from the stream to allow me and Alpha to drink without being detected, Lucky realized. *She knows we're following, but doesn't want the pups to realize. Clever Daisy!* He watched her from a distance, a warm tug of affection at his chest.

As the Sun-Dog eased himself lower in the sky, Daisy and the pups settled down for no-sun in the shelter between two rocks, under the small green leaves of a bowing tree. It would be some time before the sky was black, but Daisy seemed reluctant to go any farther, and the pups were more than happy to flop down onto the ground after walking for the entire journey of the Sun-Dog.

Not far away, Lucky and Alpha found a shaded spot beneath a low tree with branches that trailed down like pup-tails. Lucky was grateful to Daisy for having chosen to stop and make camp. *The pups must be exhausted,* he thought. *She's making sure they preserve their strength.* That warm feeling coursed through him for the kind-hearted little dog and the pups in her charge. It vanished when he turned back to Alpha.

The dog-wolf yawned, baring his huge, pointed fangs. He stretched out his forepaw and licked the livid scar.

"How did it happen?" asked Lucky, looking at the wound. "How did you get in a fight with Fierce Dogs?"

Alpha drew his paw toward him and snarled. "Why do you want to know? Do you enjoy hearing about my weakness? Is that it?"

"Of course I don't *enjoy* it!" Lucky whined, struggling to control his voice. He looked out toward the rock shelter where Daisy and the pups had made a camp. *If they hear me, they'll know we've tricked them. They'll never forgive me.* His eyes trailed back to the dog-wolf. *Anyway, what will it help to provoke Alpha?* He spoke again in a gentler voice. "I just want to understand why you hate Fierce Dogs so much."

"I don't wish to talk about it," Alpha growled. "Especially not with you, City Dog!" He tossed his head. "Why do you have so much faith in these pups? Everyone knows they're killers."

"I have faith in the *Pack*," Lucky told him. "With the right support, even young Fierce Dogs can learn to be good. Look how well they're responding to Daisy."

"I'm impressed that you think so highly of the Pack," said Alpha, relaxing onto his side. "But the truth is, a dog never changes. I've been around long enough to know that. Look at you—you're a Lone Dog; it's in your blood."

Lucky grew cold and his hackles started rising. He took a deep breath and fought the impulse to snarl back at Alpha.

The dog-wolf went on: "Your Lone Dog nature will always get the better of you. First you joined the Leashed Dogs, then the Wild Pack. Now you have taken it upon yourself to foster the

Fierce Dogs. I doubt your commitment will last. I'll wake up one morning to discover you've deserted the Pack, including your precious Fierce Dogs. We'll be left to pick up the pieces." He stared at Lucky as if silently inviting him to rise to the goading—to fight back.

I won't give him the satisfaction, Lucky thought, turning his face away and trying to hide the disgusted curl of his lip.

There was no point trying to reason with this half wolf.

Alpha yawned again. "The problem with you, Lucky, is that—"

Crash!

The sound of branches breaking had both dogs leaping to their paws, their ears pricking and bodies tensing. Beyond some nearby pines, the thump of heavy, lumbering paws rose through the dusty soil. Hackles up, Lucky watched as a dark mass shifted between the trees. From the noise it was making, and the snatches of movement, he knew it had to be huge. He sniffed, catching its thick, musty scent. He heard another crash as whatever it was shoved more branches aside. Spraying the air with pine needles, the thing burst out from the tree cover and stumbled onto the rock plane.

The beast was many times larger than the biggest dog Lucky had ever seen. Its fur was black, thick, and shaggy and it thumped its paws as it moved. Its body was broad and tailless. A giant head was covered in the same shaggy, black fur, with round ears, small, angry eyes, and a snout the color of scorched earth.

Fear shuddered through Lucky's body. "What is it?" he gasped. He could barely breathe.

Alpha was frozen to the spot, his eyes wild. "A giantfur! They live in forests and hunt alone. They are stronger than the fiercest dogs. Even wolves are scared of them!"

Thankfully the beast had not noticed Lucky and Alpha. He turned with lumbering strides, moving toward the white ridge.

Lucky's breath caught in his throat. *Daisy and the pups!* He spun around, looking Alpha in the eye. "I know this wasn't part of the plan, but we must wake Daisy! She and the pups are in terrible danger!"

He made a move toward the white ridge but Alpha leaped ahead, blocking Lucky with his broad, wolfish body.

"You're not going anywhere!" the dog-wolf snarled.

CHAPTER SEVENTEEN

"What do you mean? What are you talking about?"

Lucky tried to push past Alpha, but a paw sent him reeling back. "We have to help them! Don't you understand? What's wrong with you?"

The horror made Lucky's heart thump through his chest. There wasn't a moment to waste!

The wolf-dog gave a cruel laugh. "This has worked out even better than I'd hoped. Now we'll see what the Fierce Dog pups are *really* made of. Let them face this challenge alone."

"No, I—" Lucky began, but Alpha gave such a ferocious snarl that his words dried up.

"That wasn't a request, City Dog. That was an *order.*" His yellow gaze traveled over Lucky's back at the retreating giantfur as it plunged through the foliage. Alpha's eyes lit up. "We'll see the true nature of those Fierce Dogs." His gaze came back to settle on

Lucky. "Are you worried that their nature is a savage one?"

Lucky shook his coat and glared at Alpha. "What worries me is whether they will live or die." He hadn't felt so helpless in a long while. Had he rescued the pups just so that he could stand by and watch as they were mauled?

The giantfur trod heavily toward the white ridge. Before the beast had reached the two rocks where the dogs had settled to rest, Daisy's small face poked out, eyes wild with fear. The giantfur paused, turning its head this way and that, sniffing the air. Lucky noticed the long, jagged claws at the end of each huge paw.

Don't challenge him, Daisy! Lucky willed. His eyes flicked up to the sky. Which Spirit Dog could protect Daisy and the pups? He sent a silent message: *Spirit Dogs. Dogs of the day and of the night; dogs of water and of earth; please protect my friends. I beg you!*

Grunt suddenly appeared at Daisy's side, growling at the giantfur, his short tail standing upright.

"Get back!" Daisy ordered, but the pup ignored her, standing by her side as Lick and Wiggle huddled just behind them.

Watching from a distance, Lucky pleaded with Alpha. "We have to help them! We can't leave them to face this danger alone!"

"Yes, we *can*," Alpha snarled, square on to Lucky. "I've told you. This is an important test for the savage pups."

The giantfur took a few steps forward and stopped. It dropped its head, sniffing the dusty earth, ignoring Grunt, who had started to bark in his high-pitched pup-voice.

Without warning, the beast bounded toward Daisy and the pups. The dogs scrambled away, cowering around the rock as the giantfur roared and threw himself up on his hind legs. Even Grunt moved out of the way, darting next to the base of a pine tree.

The giantfur raised a huge paw, but instead of lashing out at the dogs, he swiped the branches of the bowing tree, sending a storm of leaves through the air. His ragged claws sank into what looked like a nub of yellow bark and emerged sparkling in amber liquid. He stuffed his paw in his mouth and sighed, a dreadful, rumbling sound. In a moment a blizzard of bees swarmed over the beast's face and he shook his head, his round ears twitching. Licking the last drop of amber juice from his claws, the giantfur took another swipe at the tree as the bees buzzed around him in a frenzied cloud.

Lucky shuddered with relief. "He's not interested in the dogs," he sighed. "Look, he's ignoring them. There's something in that tree he likes; that's what he's after."

Alpha didn't reply, his eyes fixed on the giantfur.

Lucky began to relax. *They're going to be fine. As long as Daisy and the pups keep calm, nothing will—*

Grunt stepped out behind the giantfur as Daisy, Lick, and Wiggle cowered against the rocks.

Lucky felt a tremble of dread. *What's he doing?*

"Get back here, Grunt!" Daisy urged the pup, who was squaring up to the beast.

"I'm not scared of him!" Grunt barked, stalking forward. "I don't care how big he is!"

"That pup is a fool," Alpha snarled.

Lucky tried desperately to keep calm. "Please, Alpha, we have to help! He's young; he doesn't know what he should do. He needs the help of senior dogs in the Pack—dogs like you."

Alpha tossed his head dismissively. "Fierce Dogs are unruly mutts! I told you that right from the start." He held his stance, refusing to let Lucky pass. "We must let this play out."

Daisy was pleading with Grunt to stand down. "You're just making him angry!" she yapped.

"A dog never backs down in the face of the enemy!" barked Grunt.

"A wise dog knows when it's best to avoid a fight," Lucky heard

Daisy warn him. "You can't win against a creature this big—none of us can!"

"She's right," barked Lick. "Look at the size of him! And you're just making him angry!"

As though to prove Daisy's point, the giantfur finally turned to Grunt, his eyes glistening as he stared down at the pup.

No. Oh, no. Lucky tried to dart forward, but Alpha moved again, blocking his path. He had to crane to see over Alpha's back.

The giantfur reared back on his hind legs. He swiped his fore-paws in the air, claws glinting. One paw still oozed with amber liquid. He threw back his huge head and roared, revealing a dark red mouth framed by long, yellow fangs.

The beast took a thumping step toward Grunt, who cringed and backed into Daisy and his littermates. The dogs were cornered against a wall of rock.

Lucky was sick with fear. His heart thundered in his chest. "Please, Alpha! We *have* to help them! Even if you think nothing of the pups, do it for Daisy! She's always been a loyal Pack dog; she accepted this mission without complaint, and has done her best by you and the others. She does not deserve this! We *can't* abandon her!"

Alpha's ears pricked up and his body tensed as he watched Daisy and pups cower. The giantfur towered over them, then lunged forward, a giant forepaw slicing the air. Daisy let out a short howl and rolled away, dragging the pups with her. When they climbed back to their paws, Lucky could see a trickle of blood in Daisy's fur where the giantfur's claw had snagged her skin. The giantfur roared again, and Lucky felt sure he could hear the sound of delight.

Daisy was looking around desperately and now her glance came to rest on Lucky and Alpha.

Feeling his stomach shrivel with shame, Lucky shoved himself up against Alpha. His voice was hoarse with desperation now. "What will your Pack think if you allow a loyal dog to die for no reason?"

The half wolf's tail twitched.

Near the white ridge, Daisy howled in despair. "Help! We're trapped!"

Something passed across Alpha's face—a shadow of doubt. "Fine. Follow my lead." He bounded toward the giantfur, Lucky close behind him.

Lucky slowed as he approached. He kept his stance low as the giantfur spun around and stared at him. Trembling by the wall of rock, Daisy and the pups whined with gratitude.

Alpha stepped closer, level with Lucky. His gaze was steady and his stance spoke of quiet pride. The giantfur's eyes narrowed as he inspected the Pack leader. Alpha stood his ground, refusing to move or attack. Lucky had to admire how clever he was. The half wolf was making it clear that he did not want a fight, but that he would not back down, either. Slowly, surely, he began to circle the giantfur in order to stand in front of Daisy and the pups, signaling that he would protect them. Lucky came to stand beside him.

The giantfur watched, but made no move to get closer. Lucky started to speak in a soft, gentle voice. "Daisy, when I say so, start taking small steps back along the rock wall, away from the giantfur. The same goes for you pups—just very small steps. Not yet," he warned, as he saw Wiggle panic and turn to run along the side of the rock. Wiggle froze.

"Only when Lucky says so," Daisy confirmed. Standing alongside her, Lick dipped her head in acknowledgment. Even Grunt was silent.

"Omega and I will take small steps back too," Alpha said,

not taking his eyes off the giantfur. "Nothing sudden that could alarm him."

Lucky gave a nod. "Just give the signal."

The giantfur was still glaring between Alpha and Lucky. He lifted one forepaw.

"Now!" urged Alpha.

"Remember, small steps!" Lucky whined, struggling to keep his voice quiet. He and Alpha started creeping away from the giantfur. Daisy took her cue to shuffle along the wall, Lick and Wiggle following her. Grunt made no move to withdraw. He seemed rooted to the spot, his little body rippling with tension.

The giantfur watched as Alpha and Lucky retreated. He seemed to have forgotten about the other dogs by the rocks. He lowered his muzzle and licked his paw, sucking off every last speck of amber liquid. After a moment he dropped down onto all fours with a thud. Then he turned toward the forest and started plodding away.

"He's leaving!" whispered Lucky, his body flooding with relief.

Alpha wasn't so quick to celebrate. "Not if your Fierce Dog stops him. . . ."

Grunt was stepping forward, barking: "Get out of here! You're no match for dogs! The enemy never wins against a true warrior!"

Lucky could hardly believe what he was seeing. The pup had obviously taken the giantfur's retreat as a sign of weakness. "No, Grunt!" he yelped, but the little dog ignored him.

"See what happens if you try to come back!" Grunt was barking.

"Silence, pup!" Alpha snarled.

The giantfur stopped in his tracks and spun around, his eyes fixed on Grunt. He rose onto his hindpaws once more, flexing his claws, then lunged over the pup and roared so loud that the whole world seemed to rumble with a curious thunder. Lucky dove toward Grunt and dragged the pup away from the giantfur.

"Let's get out of here!" he barked, not caring how loud his voice was now. "Run to the camp! Go!"

"This way!" Alpha barked to Daisy. He bolted around the rocks and she ran after him, glancing back to make sure that Lick and Wiggle were close behind. They scampered this way and that through the rocks, and wound their way back into the forest, disappearing between tree trunks and thickets of green foliage.

Lucky was farther back, half pushing and half dragging the reluctant Grunt. The giantfur dropped to its paws and roared once again, turning its head and rolling back its lips. Its yellow fangs were covered in slobber. Lucky's heart shuddered with fear as he and Grunt got closer to the forest. The beast's paws thumped the ground as it gave chase, gaining on them. Then, almost as suddenly as it had turned on the dogs, the beast stopped. Lucky risked a glance back and saw the giantfur sniffing the air. It followed its nose in another direction.

Lucky dropped Grunt and collapsed beneath a tree, his flanks heaving. He turned angrily on the pup. "What were you thinking? You could have gotten yourself killed! And what about the others—don't you care what happens to them?"

Grunt was unapologetic. "I'm not scared of bullies!" he growled. "You *never* back down before the enemy!"

Lucky noticed that Grunt's growl had grown deeper. There was a ruthless look to his eyes that Lucky hadn't seen before. *He's less of a pup every day.*

"You could have gotten us all killed," Lucky told the pup. He couldn't believe he needed to say this. "Your behavior was reckless. It's good not to be scared of bullies, but it is foolish to pick fights with them. The giantfur was bigger than the rest of us put together! You need to think before you go charging in like that. Hasn't Daisy taught you anything today? Do you think she's proud of you now?"

Grunt's eyes shifted to the ground. He at least had the decency to look ashamed. Lucky felt the anger drain out of him. How could he begin to explain to this young dog that he was being manipulated by Alpha—that he had walked into danger only because the half wolf wanted him to?

He sank his head against the grass, closing his eyes and wondering if Alpha could have been right.

Maybe there was no hope for the Fierce Dog pups after all.

CHAPTER EIGHTEEN

A day later, when the Sun-Dog was reaching the highest point in his journey, the Pack assembled in the meadow not far from the sloping hill. The sweet scent of pines and warm earth mingled in the air, lifting on a gentle breeze. Lucky glanced back at the rocks that lined the edges of the forest. He pictured Grunt, Lick, and Wiggle, who were taking a nap in the main part of the cave with Dart watching over them. Lucky had listened as Alpha had instructed her to keep the "vicious Fierce Dogs" away from Nose and Squirm, who were resting in the pup den. He could accept that Grunt had behaved badly and needed to learn his lesson, but to condemn Lick and Wiggle in the same breath seemed deeply unfair.

He turned back to the Pack. A short distance away, Spring was talking quietly to Snap. Lucky heard the words *aggressive* and *untrustworthy* and his tail drooped. Daisy crept close to him and

Mickey sat nearby, nodding at Lucky supportively.

Most of the dogs will side with Alpha, he thought, catching Sweet watching him.

She turned away as Alpha appeared between the pine trees, sauntering down the stoop toward the gathering, taking his position at the center.

"No doubt you will all be interested in the result of our test," he began, casting his cool eyes around the Pack. "Some of you have probably already heard about the giantfur."

A ripple of fear passed through the dogs.

"Did you actually *see* a giantfur?" asked Spring. "Do they really exist?"

Moon was on her paws. "Where was it?" She threw a nervous glance back at the rocks and the entrance to the cave.

"Nowhere near here," Alpha assured her. He scratched his ear and waited for calm. When the dogs were silent again, he continued: "We saw this monster while we were tracking Daisy and the pups. It seemed to be feeding from a tree."

"They eat *trees*?" asked Fiery, his dark face registering confusion. "Don't they like meat?"

"I am not here to discuss the giantfur," Alpha growled

impatiently. "The beast was huge. It walked close to where Daisy had settled the pups. But it wasn't interested in them. Isn't that right?"

Alpha directed this comment to Daisy, who dipped her head. "It's true; the giantfur ignored us at first. He just wanted to get to the tree. We were fine as long as we didn't get in his way."

"And *then* what happened?" asked Alpha.

Lucky tensed. This was unfair—the half wolf's questions *seemed* innocent and unthreatening. But he was actually guiding Daisy into saying things that would reflect badly on the pups. Yet again, Lucky was impressed by how clever Alpha was—even as he hated the Pack leader's tactics. He clamped his jaw shut to keep from barking in frustration.

Daisy glanced at Lucky, nervously licking her lips.

"No point turning to Omega," Alpha snarled before catching himself. His eyes darted around as if he was checking who'd noticed his lapse into anger. He took a deep breath and when he continued, his voice was calm. "Just tell the Pack the truth. What happened then?"

Daisy dropped her gaze and spoke down toward her paws. "Grunt started barking, challenging the giantfur."

There were cries of astonishment from the dogs.

"Reckless," Alpha confirmed. "A foolish choice that only a naturally vicious dog would make."

"Despicable," agreed Whine, bowing to the dog-wolf obsequiously.

Lucky couldn't bear to hear any more of this. "Or *brave*," he barked. It was true—Grunt *had* been reckless—but he would not see the pups rejected because of a momentary mistake. Grunt and the others needed time to learn; that was all. "They will grow to be great assets to the Pack, protecting it from intruders. You surely *must* see their potential."

Alpha snarled at him. "Protecting yourself is one thing, but causing a fight is another. They *wanted* a conflict. They couldn't help themselves! Particularly that nasty little Grunt. He's growing up fast and showing real malice. What dog in their right mind would chase after that sort of beast when the danger had passed?"

"He *chased* it?" Spring howled.

Lucky glared at her. Standing next to Spring, Bruno's eyes widened, although he had the good sense to stay quiet.

"Are you sure that the beast was retreating?" asked Bella carefully. "Maybe—"

"It *was* retreating," snapped Alpha. He glared in Daisy's direction, and she nodded sadly.

"You see?" Alpha went on. "Fierce Dogs can't be trusted!"

Lucky's muscles clenched with frustration. *This is not fair! How can Alpha throw the pups out of the Pack after putting them in this danger in the first place?* He looked desperately around the circle of dogs, trying to work out who among them was on his side. Spring was looking fiercely angry, and Snap's ears and shoulders drooped sadly—but were either of those good things? Every dog seemed lost in his own thoughts. Even Martha's face wasn't easy to read. Her eyes seemed to stare at nothing.

Alpha rose to his paws. "The question now is what to do with the Fierce Dogs. Do we move on and leave them in the wild, or do we"—his wolfish ears twitched—"end this?"

Lucky's jaw fell slack.

"You can't really mean . . . *kill* the pups?" Mickey yapped.

Alpha was calm and unapologetic. "It's an option."

"We'd have to do it quickly," said Snap. "They're already getting big."

"They're pups!" Lucky yelped. "How can you even *think* of hurting them?"

"I won't allow it!" howled Martha, stepping forward. She had stayed silent as the other dogs squabbled, but now her dark face was twisted with emotion. "I'll leave with them. You won't have to worry about the pups after that! But if you try to hurt them you will have to go through me!"

Alpha spun around to snarl at her, and Mickey took a step toward the water-dog, licking her neck and urging her to back down. He turned to Alpha, his voice soft and reasonable. "The pups don't mean any harm. We'll make sure that they behave. It's just a question of training."

"It's too late for that," Fiery barked. "One of them attacked Squirm. He might have killed her!"

"That was a misunderstanding," Martha growled back at him. Several other dogs backed away, afraid to get between the two massive dogs. "He was play-fighting, that's all."

"And it was only Grunt," murmured Daisy. "The other two are good; they *listen* to instructions."

Moon barked over her. "Killing is so brutal. I say we leave them behind."

Spring shook her long, floppy ears. "But they will come after us. They will seek revenge and hunt us down!"

Revenge? Lucky shook his ears. Did Spring honestly think these pups were capable of wreaking their revenge?

"It's true," agreed Whine in his cringing voice. "Better to finish with the problem now and for good."

"They are not 'a problem'!" Lucky howled. He couldn't sit here and listen to this anymore. "They're pups!"

"It was wrong to trick them," said Martha, an edge to her voice. "It was unforgivable!"

A furious howl cut through the arguing Pack and the dogs froze, shocked into silence. Standing several long-strides away were Grunt, Lick, and Wiggle.

Dart was behind them, trembling. "They heard barking . . . they wanted to know what was going on. I couldn't stop them."

Grunt unleashed a volley of angry barks: "You let the giantfur get close just to test us?" He glared at Alpha. "How could you do that? What if he had eaten us alive?"

Alpha didn't flinch at the pup's frenzied barking. "Quiet, runt! I am the leader here, in case you hadn't noticed," he shot back. "The giantfur was not part of my original plan, but yes, I did take that opportunity to see how you Fierce Dogs would react to danger. I was protecting my Pack. Such responsibility weighs heavily on me. I'll do whatever it takes to make sure that they're safe."

"Grunt," Lucky began in a soft growl. Even if he didn't agree with the half wolf's tactics, he'd do whatever it took to calm this situation. "I'm sure you understand—"

His words were cut short by another high-pitched bark. "How could *you* be in on this?" Lick was staring straight at Lucky. "We trusted you!"

Little Wiggle gazed at Lucky, his brown eyes wide and his short tail between his legs. Unlike his brother and sister, he spoke so quietly that Lucky only just caught his words: "I thought you liked us. I thought you were our friend."

Lucky's heart twisted with guilt. "I *am* your friend. I didn't mean for this to happen." He grappled for words, but found none that could explain what he'd done. It had never felt like betraying the young dogs—all along, he'd just been trying to do the right thing. But yes, he had helped to carry out Alpha's plan. He had let the pups down. He took a step toward them, looking from Grunt to Lick, and finally to Wiggle. "I am so sorry."

Wiggle turned to his litter-sister. "They *did* save us," she said. "Lucky and Alpha, they distracted the giantfur. And Lucky and Mickey looked after us when we were all alone."

Lick looked at her brother, then tilted her head to look at Lucky. "We forgive you—don't we, Wiggle?"

Wiggle responded by bounding up to Lucky, who leaned over to lick him on the ears. Mickey took a step forward, calling Lick to him as the other dogs watched.

Relief coursed through Lucky's limbs. The pups had forgiven him. And they'd done it in front of the Pack, showing their maturity and ability to fit in. That they belonged. Lucky saw doubt crossing Bella's eyes. Sweet pawed the ground thoughtfully. *They're seeing another side to these pups—a gentler side.*

Only Grunt remained fixed to the spot, standing away from the Pack. Lucky looked up and met his glare.

"How about you, Grunt? Do you accept my apology?"

Please say yes. Just do whatever it takes to save this situation.

The pup rose to his full height, puffing out his chest. "I will never forgive you!" he barked. "My brother and sister are weak, but I know an enemy when I see him. Dogs that aren't like us cannot be trusted—wild, ill-bred, sneaky dogs without any pride or honor. We should *never* have followed you." He turned to Lick and Wiggle with a growl. "You two! We're leaving!"

Lick took a step toward Grunt but hesitated, turning back to Mickey. Wiggle stayed firmly at Lucky's side.

Grunt howled at them. "Come on! They don't want us here, and we're better than this shabby Pack. We're going off to find our own kind—that's where we belong!"

A shadow fell over the assembled dogs. Lucky spun around to see a large black shape at the base of the pine trees. Dark eyes glinted above a glossy face, jaws parted with a flash of white.

The voice was brutal. "You don't need to find us. . . . We've found *you*."

CHAPTER NINETEEN

The Fierce Dog raised her muzzle and glared down at the Wild Pack. Her coat gleamed, rippling over her taut, muscular body. Dizzying fear gripped Lucky's stomach. It was the dog called Blade—the Alpha of the brutal Pack. He remembered her from the Dog-Garden—remembered her angry barks and her ferocious leadership. Standing a few paces away, Bella whimpered: "It's her! We escaped her once and she's come looking for us. She wants revenge!"

"I don't think it's us that she wants," Lucky said, nuzzling Wiggle protectively. He pushed the pup behind him, putting his body between Wiggle and Blade.

"What is it? What's happening?" Wiggle asked, trying to see around Lucky.

"Keep still," Lucky murmured, keeping his face toward Blade. Whatever happened now, it wasn't going to be good.

The long grass parted at Blade's sides and more black-and-brown faces appeared, the dogs standing in formation along the edge of the pine trees. *All the Fierce Dogs are here!*

Dart was the first to cry out. "We're under attack!"

Panic erupted in the meadow. Whine howled with fear, backing into Bruno. Bruno smacked into Snap, who leaped into the air with a volley of high-pitched barks. Only Sweet moved protectively to the front of the Pack, but Lucky could see her flank heaving with tension as she howled:

"Take position!"

Lucky shivered. The Fierce Dogs formed a neat group behind Blade, three to a row, their pointed ears perfectly aligned. That was a Fierce Dog trick through and through.

The Pack all looked toward Alpha, waiting for his order. Alpha hesitated as if he was just as unnerved by Blade's display of discipline as Lucky.

Bella charged forward, her lips pulled back into a defiant snarl. "You heard her!" she barked. "Form a line! Let Alpha and Beta through, and protect the pups!"

Lucky's heart swelled as the Pack scrambled into a loose group in front of the three pups. But Bruno and Whine were frenzied with fear and didn't listen; they spun around chaotically, yelping.

Their panic was catching and Spring pawed back and forth on the spot while Sunshine trembled beside her. Alpha started moving toward Sweet, but froze when his yellow eyes fell on Blade. Lucky caught the flash of panic on his wolfish face. *Is he going to fall apart, like he did when the black cloud appeared?*

"Dogs! Group!" boomed Blade in her powerful voice. The Fierce Dogs responded immediately, flowing around her and spilling down from the trees to the meadow.

"We have to defend the camp!" Bella howled, bravely holding her position alongside Sweet at the front of the Pack.

"We won't be defeated!" Sweet barked.

Lucky watched as the Fierce Dogs marched across the meadow. Their square faces were set, but their mouths were closed. He remembered how disciplined the dogs had been in their attack at the Dog-Garden, when they had caught the Leashed Dogs unknowingly stealing their food. If they were going to fight out in the open now, Lucky knew it was no good for his Pack to be running around, panicked.

They needed to gather their wits—and fast.

Alpha rose to his full height, his yellow eyes meeting Lucky's. *He'll hold me responsible for this,* thought Lucky. *I brought the pups to the camp, I convinced Mickey to help me . . .*

"Pack! Be *still!*" Alpha commanded in a wolfish howl. Martha trod over Daisy, who yipped, twisted, and bumped against Moon, but the panic in their eyes subsided a little.

Lucky saw Sweet edge up to Moon. "Hurry back to the rocks," she murmured. "Keep Nose and Squirm inside the pup den; don't let them come out until it's over." Moon gave a quick, grateful nod, glanced at Fiery, and then bounded away in the direction of the rocks.

The Fierce Dogs were still advancing, their unhurried steps perfectly matched so that they looked like a solid wall of black-and-brown fur. The Wild Pack stood their ground but Lucky knew they weren't prepared for this. Dart hid her head in her paws, whining helplessly. Bruno was yelping. The air around the camp seemed to have been replaced with fear-scent.

The stench was making Lucky dizzy.

Wiggle? Where's Wiggle? he thought suddenly, his guts clenching. He had lost the pup in all the panic. He couldn't see *any* of the younger Fierce Dogs.

"Pack!" barked Blade. "Contain the mutts—and *find* the pups!"

Before any of the Wild Pack could move to stop them, the Fierce Dogs' line split and they looped around the Wild Pack, hemming them in.

"Face out!" Sweet barked. "Don't take your eyes off them!" The Wild Pack backed against one another, jostling and shoving in their desperation to avoid the menacing Fierce Dogs. Lucky could feel other dogs squirming beside him and even the nip of some dog's teeth on his coat—a Packmate, driven wild by fear.

"Keep your wits," Alpha howled, "or I'll tear your throats myself!"

Suddenly the Fierce Dogs froze in formation. Looking around and gulping for air, Lucky was astounded by how easily they had gained control of the Wild Pack. Lick, Wiggle, and Grunt huddled together at the center of the circle.

Lucky squeezed through to them. "Pups, are you okay?" It was difficult to make himself heard above the desperate whines and howls, and the occasional huge bark of a Fierce Dog.

Wiggle nuzzled against him and Lick spoke up. "Yes, but what's happening?"

Grunt pulled away, glaring at Lucky. "What's happening is that *our* Pack has come to take us away. We can finally leave this horrible place, with these dishonest dogs."

Lucky winced, as though he'd been struck. "Grunt—"

The pup ignored him and thrust between the scrum of Wild Dogs, pushing his way out. Lucky bounded after him. He caught up just as Grunt reached the edge of the group.

"Stay back!" Lucky urged, blocking Grunt with his body. Then he looked up, a cold chill shuddering down his spine. The furious eyes that met his were familiar. It was Blade's Beta.

"They're here, Alpha!" he howled. "This mutt has brought them to us."

"Good work, Mace!" Blade barked. She still towered over the Packs from her vantage point at the pine trees.

"As you commanded, Blade!" he barked back, his sour breath in Lucky's face. Lucky noticed that Mace had grown sinewy. There was a sharpness to his cheeks and a wiriness to his muscles that hadn't been there when he'd encountered him in the Dog-Garden. Away from the longpaws' feeding routines, the dog had become lean and hungry—it only made him more fearsome.

Blade bounded down to the meadow and looked along the Wild Pack, her snout crinkling. "Pathetic mongrels! See how easily you are brought to submission?" Bruno and Dart whimpered in fear as she slowly circled the Wild Dogs.

Lucky trembled as she drew nearer to him. He felt movement behind him and Alpha appeared at his side. The half wolf seemed perfectly calm, even though his Pack was utterly at the mercy of the Fierce Dogs. Only Lucky could see the rapid movement of his chest as his breath came in pants.

Alpha squared up to Blade as she trod closer. "Why are you here?" he asked, his growl low and even — neither submissive nor aggressive.

Blade took a step closer and looked Alpha up and down. He was taller than she was, but she was broader, her muscles flexing beneath her glossy coat. "You *stole* our pups," she snarled.

Lucky felt Grunt push against him but he held firm, remembering the Mother-Dog that he had buried. *I heard her crying out for help. These dogs killed her,* he reminded himself. His gut churned with dread. What would these Fierce Dogs do to her pups?

Alpha held Blade's gaze. "We did not steal them. Our Omega found them alone and abandoned. He brought them here so that they could be taken care of. He thought your Pack had left your camp for good."

Blade turned her dark eyes on Lucky. "You! You broke into our camp once before, you filthy rat! Why did you take the pups?"

Lucky's legs trembled and it was all he could do to return her gaze. "I did not mean to cause any conflict. They were starving, and we . . . I . . . just wanted to help them."

"The camp had *not* been abandoned!" barked Blade. "The pups belong with their Pack. They *will* follow me."

Standing behind him, Grunt seemed to relax, as though he had expected the Fierce Dogs to come for them all along. He bounded up to Blade. "I'm here!" he barked in a high voice. "Reporting for duty."

Blade nodded with satisfaction. Lucky watched, his ears low. Had Grunt always been waiting for this moment? Was there nothing he liked about Lucky and the Wild Pack?

Lucky hoped that Grunt's ready defection would satisfy Blade, but he doubted it. *She spoke of pups—she wants* all *of them.*

"And the others?" she barked, confirming his fears.

A deep yelp broke from the circle of dogs. Martha raised her large, gentle head. "Alpha, you can't let her kidnap the pups! We promised to protect them!"

The half wolf turned to Martha, fixing her with a hard stare. "I will do what is right for the Pack," he replied. He turned back to Blade. "Take them."

Martha barked angrily. "How could you hand them over to *her*? She'll hurt them! Don't you see?"

Lucky watched, feeling a rare pang of sympathy for Alpha. What could he do? Surrounded by so many Fierce Dogs, he could not afford to challenge them.

Blade ignored Martha, turning to Lucky. "You are fortunate

that our only interest is in the pups. I *might* have taken the opportunity to chew out your tongue, mongrel dog, for tricking me in my own camp! I still might if you get in my way." Her lip twitched, a flicker of white fang flashing threateningly. "Where are the other two? I want my pups back."

Lucky's ears pricked up. Was Blade claiming to be their Mother-Dog?

Alpha narrowed his eyes. "If they are your pups, they *must* go with you."

There was a murmur of agreement from the Wild Dogs. Lucky's head cocked as he wondered: *If Blade is their Mother-Dog, then who did we bury in the garden?*

"Yes. The pups *should* be with their Mother-Dog," said Moon, relaxing her stance.

"It's natural," Snap agreed. "It isn't right to separate them. They belong with their own kind."

Sweet watched through narrowed eyes. "I thought the Mother-Dog was dead?"

So did I, Lucky thought. He caught Mickey's eye and he looked from him to the pups and then to Blade, his ears flat against his head.

But most of the other dogs were keen to do whatever it took to bring this situation to an end. They were not asking the questions that Lucky, Sweet, and Bella were.

"The pups *should* go to the Mother-Dog," Spring agreed, speaking quickly.

"It would be best," said Bruno, "for them to be with their own kind."

Lucky wrestled with the urge to call Blade a liar. What use would it do? Most of the Wild Pack had been suspicious of the pups even before Alpha's test, and Grunt had already defected. Now, surrounded by Fierce Dogs, what choice did any of them have but to agree to their enemies' demands?

The air was shattered by a sharp howl from Blade. "Give me my pups! I've waited long enough!" She bounded around the circle of dogs and launched herself at Daisy. Caught off guard, Daisy tried to spin around but couldn't escape in time.

Blade clamped her massive jaws around Daisy's neck. The little dog froze, her eyes wild with terror as the Fierce Dog Alpha pinned her to the ground with her strong forepaws.

"I want my pups back *right now!*" Blade barked. As she twisted her neck to look at Lucky, he spotted a fang-shaped white mark just below her ear. He remembered the dead pup that he and

Mickey had buried alongside the Mother-Dog. *That pup had worn the same mark on its fur.*

At his side, Mickey murmured: "The dead pup . . . Blade must be its Mother-Dog."

Lucky gave a nod. Understanding was starting to ripple through his body. "Maybe Blade's instincts are telling her that she needs pups to look after—*any* pups, as long as they're Fierce Dogs."

Lucky stared hard at the Fierce Dog. Was he looking at a mother driven wild by grief? That would certainly explain her ruthlessness—if she thought the Wild Pack had the thing she craved more than anything in the world. If she hadn't been such an expert killer, Lucky might have felt sorry for her.

He was jolted from his thoughts by Daisy's yelp. Blade's jaws had tightened around her neck.

Alpha turned to his Pack. "Let the pups go!" he commanded.

Blade gave a nod and one of the Fierce Dogs surrounding the Wild Pack stepped back to create safe, neutral space. In the center Bruno, Whine, and Dart parted to reveal Lick and Wiggle.

"Pups, go back to your Pack," Alpha told them. His words were stern but his voice was soft. Lucky thought he might have heard a hint of regret.

Lick walked past the Wild Dogs until she was standing a short distance from Blade. Her head was held high and her stubby tail pointed behind her. Lucky's heart swelled with pride. The female pup had learned and grown up so much in such a short time. With her bold, fearless nature she could have been a great asset to the Pack. But now she would be brought up to be aggressive and savage—she would have no choice but to *become* the dog that Alpha feared.

They could all have been good dogs, Lucky felt sure. *Even Grunt*... He looked at the glossy-furred pup, who joined his sister with a lick of the nose. She returned his gesture, then searched the crowd of dogs. She found Lucky's face and blinked at him sadly.

Only Wiggle held back, reluctant to join his old Pack. Martha had drawn closer to him and he backed against her, whimpering. "I don't *want* to go with them. I want to stay with you and Lucky, and Mickey and the others."

Martha looked around her, addressing all the Wild Dogs at once. "Are you *really* going to let this happen? How can you hand the pups over to these brutes?"

"Come, Dagger!" barked Mace. Blade's Beta marched forward alongside a stubby-faced Fierce Dog with lighter brown fur. The Wild Dogs fell back, allowing them to pass. Wordlessly the Fierce

Dogs flanked Wiggle, who had no choice but to walk with them.

Martha turned away with a sad whine, backing out of the circle of dogs. She ignored the Fierce Dog standing guard, loping past him through the meadow with her head bowed.

The Fierce Dogs led Wiggle to his littermates. He leaned against Lick, his ears flat. "Do we really have to go?" he whimpered.

Grunt scowled at him. "We belong with dogs like these—fierce, brave warriors—not that ragged bunch of scroungers who cower at the sight of a silly giantfur!"

Blade's ears pricked up and she cast a curious look at Lucky. The other Fierce Dogs growled, as if the giantfur was in earshot. That they were not terrified of such a beast made Lucky's tail droop in unease.

At last Blade released her grip on Daisy, who scampered away, trembling at Bella's side. "Prepare to leave!" Blade barked. The Fierce Dogs stiffened.

"I don't want to go!" Lick whined.

"Me neither," said Wiggle. "Mickey, don't let them take us!"

Mickey lowered his head. "We won't forget you," he murmured pitifully.

Blade glared at him. "One more word, fluffy pooch, and I'll rip your throat out!"

Mickey flinched. Lucky tensed by his side, preparing to fight if he had to. *If Blade touches Mickey she'll have to deal with me—even if it's the last thing I do!*

Blade lifted her muzzle, trailing her challenging gaze around the circle of dogs. Then she turned away, her body stiff and triangle ears pricked. The Fierce Dogs started marching toward the pine trees—Blade in the lead, Mace at the rear, and the pups trapped in the middle.

Lucky stood bolted to the spot, watching as the puppies were led away. *Forest-Dog, protect these pups. They're so young and innocent, and their Pack is so vicious. Please don't let them come to any harm.*

The Sun-Dog bounded above the Fierce Dogs, making his descent over the horizon. Lucky looked into the clear blue sky. How could it be so peaceful when there was so much chaos in the world beneath it? He remembered the storm that had terrified his Pup-Pack as they had cowered at their Mother-Dog's side. He thought of the mighty Sky-Dogs. Weren't they the most powerful of all the Spirit Dogs?

Lucky sent out another prayer. *Please, mighty Sky-Dogs, keep my little Packmates safe.*

Wiggle pressed to the edge of the Fierce Dog Pack so he could throw Lucky a final sad look. Lucky cocked his head, his tongue lolling from the side of his mouth. He forced his tail to wag. He hoped this was encouraging, that it would give the pup some strength for the long road ahead.

It was a struggle to find the energy not to howl or turn away. Inside, Lucky's heart was twisting in sorrow

CHAPTER TWENTY

A low mist gathered around the branches of the pine trees, drifting down to the meadow and wrapping it in a gray pelt. The Moon-Dog's light pierced through it, but the stars were invisible in the murky no-sun.

Sitting between the pine trees and staring blankly beyond the camp, Lucky shuddered. The sharp fang of the rising wind caught at his fur. Still he kept watch for the puppies who never arrived. Several times he thought he could make out their shadowy shapes bounding along the lake toward the pines. From the corner of his eye he caught a flash of their glossy coats. His ears twitched at the imagined sound of their excited yaps, the soft crunch of their paws on the earth.

Lucky sighed and sank into the long grass. The pups would be far away by now, settling down for the night with the Fierce Dogs. How would they cope with such a brutal Pack? *Even Grunt is more vulnerable than he thinks, and Lick has learned a lot, but she's still so young.*

Then there was poor little Wiggle . . .

The camp had been unusually quiet since the Fierce Dogs had left. Mickey had gone to find Martha, who sat despondently by the pup den. Fiery had led a hunting party; Spring, Dart, and Daisy had gone on patrol. They had eaten early, barely exchanging words as the food had been distributed by rank, as was the Wild Dogs' custom. Then Alpha had retreated to the cave. No one had mentioned the Great Howl and Lucky was secretly relieved. *I know it could help to make the Pack feel more whole again. But I'm not ready to share something like that with these dogs, not yet—not after they allowed the Fierce Dogs to take the pups away.* Lucky thought bitterly of how panic had broken out among the Wild Pack—while the Fierce Dogs remained calm and regimented.

We let the pups down. . . .

He scented Sweet before he saw her. She had climbed the hill to the pine trees and appeared beside him, ghostly in the mist. Lucky felt a twinge in his chest, a confused emotion that he couldn't place. He kept his gaze focused on the woods in the distance.

Sweet trod lightly and crouched beside him. "I guess you'll be off again soon."

It was more of a statement than a question, and Lucky did not reply. The mist was slowly swirling down from the branches of the pines in white loops. Sweet spoke again. "After all, you're a Lone Dog. You've said it time and again, ever since we met in the city. You just seem to end up in the Pack out of, I don't know, some sense of duty to other dogs. Last time it was for Bella and the Leashed Dogs. This time it was for the pups. Now that they've gone . . ." Her voice sounded wistful. "I know you're not a Pack Dog—not really. I won't be angry with you if you leave again. I'll understand this time. I'll forgive you."

Lucky's ears twitched and a wrinkle of irritation ran along his back. "You'll *forgive me?*" he snarled. "How thoughtful, Sweet. How generous." He turned, meeting her bright eyes, which seemed to glow in the expanding mist.

Sweet was taken aback. "I didn't mean to insult you. I just thought . . . you don't *want* to be a Pack Dog, do you?"

"What does it matter what I want?" Lucky replied. "I *wanted* to help the pups, but now they're with those savage Fierce Dogs. I didn't want to hand them over—but I did it. And for what?"

He glared at Sweet and she blinked back, looking hurt.

Lucky barked in frustration. "For the good of the Pack, that's what! Even when it went against all my instincts. You saw how rough Blade was with Daisy. And the pups are so small. I know Grunt acts tough, and Lick is bold and confident, but they are still just *pups.*" He cast a look out into the gloom, but a new bank of mist had rolled in from the lake.

"I understand how you feel about letting them go," Sweet murmured. "But the Fierce Dog Alpha said she was their Mother-Dog—surely she wouldn't hurt her own pups?"

Lucky fell silent, remembering the stiff body of the dead Mother-Dog beneath the porch. He thought again of the pup with the white fang mark on his neck. *Whether they're her pups or not, Blade seemed determined to look after them.* He knew that had to be a good sign, yet something just felt *wrong.* Why had the Fierce Dogs abandoned the pups in the first place? How had the Mother-Dog died?

"I don't know, Sweet." It was all he could say. How could he explain the tightness in his stomach or the sourness catching the back of his throat?

"So you *will* be off soon?" Sweet pressed. "I don't mind; I just . . . want you to tell me before you disappear. It would be good to get a chance to say good-bye."

Lucky turned on her angrily. "Have I said that I'm leaving?"

Sweet's narrow face was scarcely visible in the mist. "I just assumed . . . with the pups gone, why would you stay?"

"Isn't that obvious? I'll stay because I'm a Pack Dog now. Haven't I proven myself enough for you? I'm surprised you're even speaking to me. Isn't it beneath a Beta to talk to the Omega? Are you taking cover behind the mist, so no dog will see you?"

Sweet's eyes had widened with shock. "Don't be like that, Lucky. I didn't mean to offend you—"

He didn't let her finish. "But you *have* offended me, Sweet. You make me sound like I change my mind every sunup; like I'm not committed to anything, or any dog." His ears flicked back. The words spilled out of him, a swirl of bitterness and anger. He thought of Grunt, Lick, and Wiggle and his heart throbbed with loss. "Haven't I shown that I can act in the interests of the Pack? Even when it meant letting the pups go? I've tried so hard to do what's right by the Pack—not that *you've* noticed! Tonight I'll sleep out in a draft, just to remind you and the other high-ranking dogs that I'm the lowest dog, less than nothing. Even though I know there's another way to live, that dogs don't need to be punished and controlled by rank, I'm going to live like a Pack Dog—because that's what I am now."

"I know it isn't easy being Omega," Sweet said, her voice a

gentle, soothing whimper. "But rules are important—it's what gives us security. Without rules, how would we know what we should do, or how to act in a crisis?"

Lucky couldn't believe what he was hearing. He gave a sigh. "For all Alpha's rules, has the Pack performed any better? Oh, things work well enough when food is plentiful and everyone does what they're told—but look what happened when the Fierce Dogs came. The Pack fell apart! The Pack *failed*, despite all its rules."

"I knew it!" Sweet barked, her voice rising, provoked to anger at last. "I knew you would turn on the Pack sooner or later!"

Lucky glared at her, their eyes locking. The world grew silent, only the breeze shrilling on the night air, lifting and spreading the mist like clouds of dust. A wave of despair ran through him, his fur rising along his back. *I must prove to Sweet that I am a Pack Dog once and for all!*

An idea started to form. He turned to the edge of the hill and scanned the meadow. The wind had torn holes in the mist. He could see Spring and Dart walking side by side, surveying the perimeter of the camp. *No, not them . . .*

He spotted Snap treading through the long grass, returning from a hunt, the limp body of a ferret hanging from her jaws.

"Snap!" he barked loudly.

The stout hunter squinted through the mist, ears pricked. "Omega, is that you?"

He took a step forward, standing over the edge of the hill. "Omega the City Dog challenges Snap the hunter!" he barked. Sweet rose to her paws, surprise crossing her narrow face.

Lucky took a deep breath. "Do you accept the challenge?"

Snap dropped the ferret, her eyes gleaming. Her body stiffened. "I accept!" she barked.

Lucky fought down a tremor of nerves. *She wants revenge for the previous fight—the one where I beat her with trickery.*

By the time that Lucky and Sweet had reached the bottom of the hill, half the Pack had gathered in the meadow.

Moon was nursing Nose and Squirm with Fiery standing guard, and plenty of familiar faces were emerging from the mist: Mickey, Bruno, Spring, Dart. Even Martha appeared, a dark blur in the gloom as she hung back.

Alpha walked slowly out and sat in the mouth of the cave. He said nothing, but gave Sweet a nod.

He approves the fight, Lucky thought. *I bet that means he thinks I can't win. But I'm going to show him.*

Sweet stepped close to Lucky, her breath catching the fur of his ear. "Are you sure you want to do this?"

Lucky turned and met her eye. "Yes, *Beta*. I am."

She addressed the Pack. "Omega has challenged Snap to a fight, and Snap has accepted. If Omega wins, he will be promoted above her. If Snap wins there will be no change in Pack rankings." She took a step back. "May the Sky-Dogs look with blessing on your combat!" she barked. "May your fight be fair, and may the outcome be favored by the Spirit Dogs. When the battle is done, we all remain Packmates. And we all shall protect the Pack! On my word . . . *fight!*"

Snap sprang at Lucky immediately, knocking him off balance and sinking her jaws into his hind leg. He yelped and pulled away as she drew back, snarling. Hackles up, he started toward her, curling his lips over his fangs. He tried to leap at her but Snap was fast, slipping out of the way and behind him, pouncing on his back and catching his shoulder with a deep nip.

Lucky howled and shook her off roughly, throwing her to the ground. He pressed down with his forepaws, pinning her, and aiming a bite at her exposed stomach, but she scrambled out of his grip and all he managed to do was tear a shallow gash in the edge of her flank. She ducked into the mist, vanishing for a moment as Lucky blinked in confusion.

Snap's voice came from behind him. "Nice try, City Dog!"

He made a dive at her but she leaped beneath him, catching his inner leg with her forepaws and punishing him with another sharp nip. They locked in combat, scraping at each other with their claws, yelping, and biting.

The Pack started barking instructions at the fighting dogs.

"Go for her belly!" Mickey called.

"Fight him, Snap!" yelped Whine. "He's only Omega; you can beat him!"

Then Snap pulled away, panting. "One more bite and you're a dead dog!" she snarled.

"Don't speak so soon," Lucky barked. "You're half my size!"

"And twice your speed!" Snap ducked into the mist again, disappearing from view. Lucky growled, squinting. He could just make out the outline of her wiry fur.

"We'll see about that!" Lucky gathered up all his strength. *I have to win this!* he thought urgently. *I can't be Omega anymore; I have to show everyone how good a Pack Dog I can be!*

He lunged at Snap, pretending to go for her stumpy tail. At the last minute, he swung around, throwing open his jaws and aiming for her neck. Snap darted away with a yelp, leaped in the air, and launched herself at Lucky's back leg, burying her fangs into his flesh and squeezing.

Pain shot through him. Lucky howled as blood spurted from the wound. He felt it sticking to his fur. Snap would not let go. The other dogs barked excitedly as the hot, red scent rose on the air.

The mist swirling through the meadow seemed to drift inside Lucky's mind, into his eyes, blurring his vision. His pulse thundered at his temples, drowning out the frenzy of barks. The pain was dizzying and Lucky stumbled, a sickness rising in his throat.

"Enough!" howled Alpha. The dog-wolf trod toward the Pack, mist swirling around him. "The fight is over. Snap has defended the challenge."

Instantly Snap released her grip on Lucky and shrank back. A sharp jolt of pain shot up his leg—it was even worse now that she'd let go—but the wave of sickening dizziness was passing. Lucky ducked his head to lap at the wound, trying to stanch the flow of blood.

"Are you okay?" Mickey asked.

"Does it hurt?" pressed Bella, taking a tentative step toward him.

"I'll be fine," Lucky replied, his tail clinging to his flank. He wanted them to leave him alone. Alpha was already walking away, and he wished the other dogs would do the same.

Snap approached him, her tail wagging. "Now we're even," she told him with a friendly lick. All hostility was gone.

Lucky limped past the Pack, his head lowered. The shame prickling in his fur was worse than the pain of his wounds—much worse.

Sweet bounded after him. "Omega, I want to talk to you," she called. Her tail was thrashing and her eyes were shining like tiny Moon-Dogs.

Lucky kept walking as she leveled alongside him. "Why would you want to talk to me?" he murmured. "I'm still the Omega."

"Exactly," she replied. "You tried to advance and you did it by the Pack rules—and even though you lost, you aren't abandoning your position. Don't you see? That's far more proof than if you'd won. You *are* a loyal member of the Pack!" She licked his ear and he felt a tingle of warmth, a deep thrumming of happiness that rose from his chest. Then he thought of the pups out there in the darkness. He remembered Alpha's unforgiving face. He thought of Whine's mocking smile. The breeze shrilled over the meadow, and as the heat of the fight fell from his fur, Lucky felt the cold close in on him. It would be worse later as the chill of night took hold, once the rest of the Pack was warm inside the cave and he was alone in the drafty spot reserved for the Omega.

He limped steadily toward the cave, ignoring Sweet, who paused and fell behind. He winced at the pain in his sore leg, but he kept up the pace. The wind rustled the leaves of the nearby trees and played with Lucky's fur. Shivering, he reached the entrance of the cave. Before he stepped inside, he paused and threw a look over his shoulder. There was now no trace of Sweet beyond the bank of white mist.

He was all alone.

CHAPTER TWENTY-ONE

The next sunup, Lucky stepped out onto a changed meadow. The mist had cleared and the sharp breeze had faded away. The Sun-Dog shone bright in a cloudless sky. The air was clean and peaty. Insects buzzed in the long grass, hovering over small pink flowers that sprang up in bursts.

Lucky carefully stretched his back leg. It still throbbed where Snap had sunk in her teeth, and gathering water-soaked moss for Alpha and Sweet early this morning hadn't done it any good at all. But even so, the worst of the pain had faded overnight, just like the mist. He padded toward the river, where he drank thirstily. Then he sat in the shade of a tree at the edge of the forest as sunlight danced across the surface of the water. He watched from the shade as first Sweet, then Spring and Dart, stepped out of the cave and began to cross the meadow.

Heavy pawsteps approached from the forest, the crack of

breaking twigs and crumbling leaves. Rising to his paws, Lucky turned to see Bruno.

"How are you feeling today?" asked the thickset old dog.

"I'm fine," said Lucky, pushing away thoughts of the pups. They were gone now—he had to accept that.

"Alpha has called a meeting," said Bruno. "Are you coming?"

Lucky heard the chirping of birds in the branches of a tree and turned to gaze in that direction. He had a powerful impulse to wander into the forest, to follow the path of the river to wherever it led him.

That was my old life, he reminded himself. *My life as a Lone Dog, my life of freedom . . .*

He shook himself and went to join Bruno. The two of them made their way back to the meadow. Most of the dogs were already there, forming a circle around Alpha and Sweet, who stood by his side. She acknowledged Lucky with a dip of her sleek head as he and Bruno joined the gathered Pack.

Alpha had already started talking. "We will have to be better organized," he was saying. "Our standoff with the Fierce Dogs was a disgrace. Not one dog acted with sufficient discipline or bravery, except Beta"—he glanced at Sweet—"and Bella, who gave sensible commands when needed."

Bella's ears pricked up at the rare compliment from their Pack leader.

Lucky watched. This was close to an acknowledgment from Alpha that he had failed to act appropriately in the face of the Fierce Dogs. Lucky's eyes trailed to the scar on the curve of the half wolf's forepaw.

Alpha continued: "Beta ordered the Pack to take position, but instead there was panic and chaos."

Bruno dropped his head guiltily. Dart shuffled on her paws with a small whine.

Alpha's ears twitched. "I don't want to go over that now except to say that in the future, we must be much better organized, and more responsive to threats. I would like to see fighters move to the front, defenders move to the back. There will be no desertion or failure of duty!"

"The Pack is much larger than it used to be," Sweet pointed out. "Most of the dogs could probably use some training."

Alpha gave a nod. "Good idea. We should have a better system of alert and Pack formation. I will put you in charge of that."

Sweet returned the nod.

"That leaves me with another matter," said the half wolf, rising to his paws. "The Fierce Dogs came here. They know how to find us. This time they were only interested in claiming their pups. Next time we might not be so fortunate."

"What are you saying, Alpha?" asked Moon.

"I'm saying that it is time for us to leave."

"Leave?" Spring yapped. "But we just arrived!"

"This camp is perfect," added Bella. "Look how well the Pack has settled here. The hunting is good, and the cave provides us cover from the wind and rain."

"Where would we go?" asked Sunshine in a small voice.

"Back to our old camp," said Alpha. "The black cloud has passed. It should be safe."

The Pack erupted into barks, yelps, and whines.

"But that's so far away!" whimpered Sunshine. "It was such a tough journey to get here."

"We can't walk forever," agreed Whine. "We need a permanent territory."

"The old camp is closer to the Dog-Garden," Mickey pointed out. "How do we know it's safer there?"

"It's easier for us to protect," said Alpha. "Here in the meadow we're a sitting target. Anyone can spy on us from the hill—they can sneak up on us and take us by surprise. . . ."

"Not if we place a watch-dog by the pine trees," said Bella.

Daisy shuddered. "But any dog up there would be all alone, with the others down in the valley. It would be dangerous." Her eyes shot up to the pine trees. "If the dog raises the alarm, they will just be the first dog to be killed!"

Whine and Sunshine whimpered, and Dart yelped in agreement.

"Settle down!" snarled Alpha, thumping his paw impatiently. The dogs fell silent. He spoke again in a low growl. "It is dangerous here—we have *all* seen that. Our old camp was more defendable, even if it was closer to the wrath of the Sky Dogs and the Fierce Dogs. But there is another possibility." He paused, making sure all the dogs were listening. "We could travel in the other direction, over the white ridge."

Lucky saw several of the dogs visibly tense at this. Even Sweet seemed shocked, turning to watch Alpha closely.

"But what about the giantfur?" Bruno yelped.

"In the end, he was no threat," said Alpha. "He only attacked because that pup provoked him."

"There could be others out there," said Moon. "Lots of them! Packs, even!"

"Giantfurs are not Pack creatures—not from what I can tell.

They act alone." Alpha glanced pointedly at Lucky when he said this.

Lucky knew what the half wolf was implying. *Whatever he thinks, I am a Pack Dog now.*

Lucky pictured the white ridge. It had been tough terrain on the approach: parched, rocky, and unforgiving. He thought about small dogs like Whine and Sunshine—they would struggle out there. It would be even worse for Nose and Squirm. But maybe Alpha had a point—the Fierce Dogs were unlikely to stray that far, and their thick, heavyset bodies were not suited to climbing rocks.

"We didn't get a good enough look at the land beyond the white ridge," said Lucky. "It was very dry, and it might not be an easy place to make a camp. But maybe Alpha's right. I can't imagine other dogs living out there. Daisy, you got the closest of any dog. What do you think?"

All eyes turned to the little dog, but before she could reply, Sunshine let out a loud yelp. The Pack all turned to see that she was gazing up at the pine trees. She stiffened; her ears pricked up. "Someone's coming!" she barked. "I can smell them."

"Dogs?" Lucky's eyes shot up to the edge of the hill. Sunshine was right! Something *was* moving up there. His stomach clenched and he took a step forward, his eyes trained on the shivering grass beneath the pine trees. He saw a small, dark creature—too small for an adult dog—and instantly relaxed. It had to be some sort of prey.

"Yes, a dog!" yelped Sunshine. "But just one . . ."

Mickey was standing at the edge of the circle of dogs, nearer to the pine trees. "It's a pup!" he yelped.

The Pack watched in amazement as a small dog tumbled out from between the long grass and scrambled over the hill, half running, half stumbling.

It was Lick!

Lucky's heart drummed in his chest as she flung herself toward the circle of dogs. He stared into the tree line. Where were her littermates? Why was Lick alone?

"She's hurt!" Martha cried.

The big water-dog was right. Lucky watched in horror as Lick loped over to them in broken, jolting strides. Her fur was torn with multiple wounds, the metallic tang of blood mingling with her sweet, milky pup scent. She made the final stretch on trembling paws and collapsed against Mickey, who covered her in gentle licks. Martha and Lucky rushed to join them.

Alpha surveyed the scene with his pale eyes. He spoke with

surprising gentleness as he addressed Lick. "What has happened to you?"

Panting heavily, Lick broke away from Martha, Mickey, and Lucky's affectionate embrace. She took a couple of wincing steps toward Alpha. Her body was a mess of bite marks and tears, but she addressed the wolf-dog bravely.

"It was Blade!" she yelped. "She attacked us when we were on the road. She kept saying, 'You're not my real pups! You're not my real pups!'" Lick gasped, struggling to control her breath. Her small chest moved rapidly, and her whole body shook. She seemed desperate to speak, to fight her exhaustion and get the words out. "Then she killed him!" she howled. "She killed Wiggle."

Lucky's breath caught in his throat. For a moment it was as though the Sun-Dog had vanished, and the whole world was black and icy cold. He could hear Lick's voice, but saw nothing.

Then warmth returned to his cheeks and he opened his eyes. Sweet was licking him. "Lucky, are you okay?"

He gave a slow nod.

"The Fierce Dogs killed your litter-brother?" asked Alpha.

"Yes," whimpered Lick. "Blade killed him. She was going to kill Grunt, but he begged her not to. He promised that he was a real Pack Dog, and that he would earn his place. That he would be useful to her. He made her believe him. He didn't seem sorry about Wiggle at all."

Alpha lowered his head though he still towered over her. "And how did *you* get away?"

Lick gazed up at him, her eyes wide. "Blade caught me and started biting and scratching. Then, from nowhere, the air was white. One moment Blade was attacking me; the next it was like I was invisible! The whiteness covered everything and I managed to escape. I don't know what it was."

"Fog," said Alpha.

Lucky remembered how the mist had covered the land. His eyes shot up. The Sun-Dog blinked down at him—there was not a single cloud overhead. He gazed in wonder. *Thank you, Sky-Dogs. . . . You heard me; you sent the mist.*

Lick swallowed. "I could hear them following me. They were furious that I had escaped. I rubbed myself in leaves and dirt to cover my scent—just like Mickey taught us." She threw the black-and-white dog a grateful look and he took a step forward.

"You have been so brave," he told her.

"You're my Pack," she replied. She turned to Lucky, then to Alpha. "You've always been my Pack. I am not one of them. I am no Fierce Dog. This is the only place for me, and I'll do whatever it takes to fit in."

Lucky's chest burned with pride. Lick was a remarkable little dog—loyal and resilient. "You'll let her stay, won't you, Alpha?"

The wolf-dog watched Lick, then turned his yellow eyes on Lucky. "You really believe in this pup, don't you?"

"She will be a valuable Pack member," said Lucky. "She won't harm these dogs. One day she may protect us all with all her courage and passion. There is nothing to fear in letting her stay." He cocked his head, holding Alpha's gaze. "I think you see it too. Don't you?"

Lucky wanted to beg Alpha to let Lick stay—or to bark and howl, to force the dog-wolf somehow—but he controlled himself. He had to let Alpha come to his own decision.

He hates me enough to cast her out again simply to spite me.

Lucky looked around the Pack. There was only tenderness in their faces as they watched Lick. It would all come down to the will of Alpha.

Their leader raised his muzzle, staring out toward the pine trees. Then he looked the other way, beyond the cave and the forest, in the direction of the white ridge.

There was finality in Alpha's voice when he spoke again. "We have to move now; we have no choice. The Fierce Dogs will soon come after Lick. We leave today."

"I can stay?" Lick breathed in a small voice, her short tail wagging hopefully.

"You can," said Alpha. "We will see if you can be all that Omega has promised. The Pack needs loyal fighters, dogs who are brave and strong. For now, you should rest and clean your wounds. We must depart before the Sun-Dog greets the lake."

Bruno and Sunshine exchanged glances and Whine shivered. Lucky knew it would be a tough journey for these dogs, but there was nothing they could do now—Alpha had made his decision. Martha and Mickey led Lick away and the Pack dispersed, resting before the long journey ahead, bidding farewell to the peaceful meadow that had briefly been their home.

Relief flooded through Lucky's limbs. Lick was going to stay with them. *I'll do anything it takes to keep this pup safe,* he promised himself. *Even if it kills me.*

Only he and Alpha remained in the meadow. He turned to the dog-wolf. "Thank you. She won't let you down, and neither will I."

Alpha's yellow eyes were unreadable. "It will not be easy,

keeping a Fierce Dog among us. Blade will come searching for her again."

"We can get a head start if we go at once," said Lucky. "And there's an advantage in being mixed—Leashed and Wild, large and small. The Fierce Dogs all think the same way—they only know how to follow orders."

Alpha stretched out his forepaw and examined his scar. "That's all they *need* to know."

Lucky shook his fur. "There are other things. We have skills and experience. Together, we are smarter than them. We have wit and cunning. That's what you need to survive."

"I hope you're right, City Dog," said Alpha. "Because wherever we go, we will need to be one step ahead of them."

Lucky thought of the Sky-Dogs who had brought the mist. "The Spirit Dogs are on our side; I feel certain of that. We will need their help for the long journey ahead. The world changed when the longpaws left. Maybe things will change back, and the longpaws will return. Or perhaps there will be another Big Growl to change the earth again. But for now, there's only one thing we can do. We have to keep moving."

Lucky and Alpha gazed over the landscape. They had traveled long and hard to get here, and now they faced yet another journey. But at least the Pack was still together. At least Lick had returned to them. And for what it was worth, Alpha seemed to have accepted Lucky.

It was a start.

Lucky's paws crunched on the forest floor as he ran. Dappled bronze
light, scattered by the branches above him, burnished the fallen
leaves beneath his paws. Just ahead, he could see Fiery's powerful
haunches as his huge Packmate bounded through the forest.

"Lucky!" Fiery turned to bark over his shoulder. "Remember—
keep your nose alert for Blade and the others."

"Don't worry." Lucky wasn't about to forget the savage leader
of the Fierce Dogs. He felt his hackles rise as he pictured her
snarling, arrogant face. Lucky sniffed the frosty forest air for any

trace of their enemy, but all he could detect were dying leaves, running water, and tiny creatures of the earth.

No, Blade won't get near the Pack while I can stop her. . . .

"Good. Just stay alert, and make sure the others do too." Fiery swung his great head to scan the forest. "Alpha's certain Blade will be back for revenge."

"I think Alpha's right." Lucky increased his pace until he was running closely at Fiery's flank. "And he's right not to let any dog go out alone."

Fiery's muscles bunched as he slowed his pace to a trot. "Let's move carefully now," he growled. The half-wolf Alpha had insisted that Fiery go out with Lucky on this first hunt of his new status. Lucky was fairly sure that was for strength in numbers and not an indication of his leader's lingering distrust of him. It felt odd that Alpha should care about Lucky's life after all that had happened between them, but Lucky and the half wolf seemed to have reached a kind of peace.

For now.

Lucky didn't think he would ever trust Alpha completely, but that wasn't a thought he could share with Fiery. He was the Pack's third-in-command after Sweet, Alpha's Beta, and had always been deeply, fiercely loyal to their leader.

"Lucky!" The excited yelp came from a clump of grass to his left, and Lick burst into view.

"You kept up," barked Lucky, amused. "Well done."

The young Fierce Dog visibly swelled, her head lifting. Lucky's surge of pride in her was mixed with a tingle of foreboding. Though she was young, Lick's Fierce Dog heritage already showed in her powerful muscles and her glossy hide—and in that strong jaw lined with ferocious teeth. Some of the other dogs were still nervous about accepting a Fierce Dog into their Pack.

Fools. Lick's about as vicious as a rabbit.

"Keep your eyes open, Lick," he growled softly at the young dog. "Remember, it's a white rabbit we're looking for, and Dart swears she saw one around this warren."

"Why does it have to be white?" Lick frowned. "I can smell so much prey here."

Lucky's heart sank, but he kept his voice cheerful. "Alpha insists on a snow-white rabbit for the Naming Ceremony."

Lick's head lowered, and all her energy seemed to seep out of her. "Oh. For Squirm and Nose. I bet it's going to be amazing." In a resentful growl she added, "Not that I'd know anything about Naming."

"Neither do I." Lucky shunted her cheerfully with his nose. "I never had a Naming Ceremony, Lick."

"Really?" She cocked her head, seeming a little more hopeful.

"Really. I don't even remember getting my name. Sometimes there's a vague memory, but . . ." Lucky shook his shoulders. "I remember a young longpaw with yellow hair like a tail. She was in danger. I remember my Mother-Dog being pleased with me. I hear a voice saying Lucky . . . but the memory slips away just when I'm about to seize it, like a sneaky piece of prey."

Lick gave a rumbling laugh, a deep one that reminded Lucky just how fast the young dog was growing. "At least I'm not the only one, then."

"It's not something all dogs do," Lucky reminded her. "Think of the Leashed Dogs."

Lick sniffed and said wryly, "They don't know how to do anything right."

Poor Lick. She's putting on a brave face, but I know she's desperate to get her adult dog name like the others. Covering his anger at Alpha, Lucky nudged her. "You'll get a Naming Ceremony. Don't worry."

"I hope so." Lick scowled. "Why won't Alpha let me have one now?"

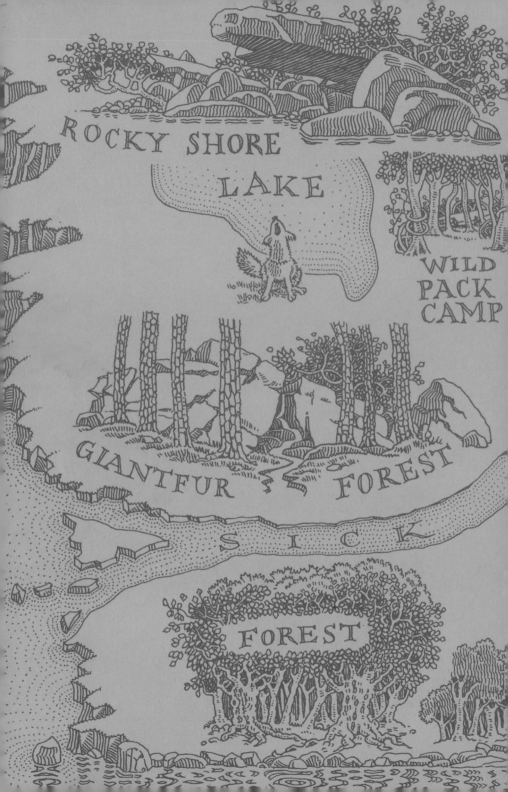